DANDELION

DANDELION

JEAN URE

HarperCollins *Children's Books*

First published in the United Kingdom by
HarperCollins *Children's Books* in 2022
HarperCollins *Children's Books* is a division of HarperCollins*Publishers* Ltd
1 London Bridge Street
London SE1 9GF

www.harpercollins.co.uk

HarperCollins*Publishers*
1st Floor, Watermarque Building, Ringsend Road
Dublin 4, Ireland

1

ISBN 978-0-00-849810-8

Jean Ure asserts the moral right to be identified
as the author of this work

A CIP catalogue record for this title is available from the British Library

Typeset in Gill Sans 12/20pt by
Palimpsest Book Production Ltd, Falkirk, Stirlingshire

Printed and bound in the UK using 100% renewable electricity
at CPI Group (UK) Ltd

For Madelaine Ford and Katie McLoughlin,

two very good readers

CHAPTER
1

Something very odd happened to Lily as she walked to school one morning. She was approaching the corner of Barclay Road when a strange girl suddenly appeared. Simply sprang out in front of her from nowhere. Lily stopped automatically. The girl stood, staring. Lily stared back. It wasn't polite to stare, but it also wasn't polite to jump out in front of a person. And what *did* it think it looked like? All dressed up as if for a party, with a green sparkly top made out of bits of shiny stuff, and purple tights with orange swirls. Orange swirls! As if purple wasn't bad enough. Who went round like that at eight o'clock in the morning? *And* painted its lips purple to go with its tights. *And* had bright yellow hair all sticking up in a frill like a dandelion. *And* was still subjecting Lily to its ill-mannered gaze. It deserved to be stared at!

'Hm!' The girl crinkled her forehead. 'You are Lily O'Grady, aren't you?'

Lily wished, afterwards, that she had said 'Why?' Or even more to the point: 'And who are you?' But of course she didn't; her brain was still too busy trying to work out where this strange ungracious creature had come from.

'So are you?' said the strange ungracious creature. 'Or aren't you?'

Reluctantly, Lily admitted that she was.

'Oh, rats!' The girl threw up her hands in exasperation. 'Try again!'

And with that, she was gone. No 'excuse me'. No 'sorry'. No kind of explanation. Just 'Try again!' and disappeared.

Except that no one ever just disappeared. Not suddenly like that. Any more than they just appeared, out of seemingly nowhere. She must have been hiding behind a tree, or a – a hedge. Or something. Waiting for Lily to come walking by on her way to school so that she could spring out and surprise her. But why? Why would she do that? And how did she know Lily's name? It was a mystery!

She could hardly wait to get to school and tell the others. For once, she had something really exciting to report. Even Geraldine could hardly fail to be impressed!

As a rule, Lily had the journey to school timed to perfection. By walking really fast she could arrive just as the first bell was ringing, giving her the chance to chat with Geraldine and Tara before classes began. Today, having spent precious minutes peering down Barclay Road in a vain attempt to spot places where someone might be able to hide, she found the second bell was already ringing as she went panting through the gates.

Miss Hancock was standing there, beetle-browed, checking latecomers.

'Cutting it a bit fine, aren't we, Lily? Hurry along now! Everyone else has gone in.'

Thanks entirely to that ridiculous Dandelion Head! Although, of course, it had to be said, it was only because of Dandelion Head that she had a story to tell in the first place. A really good one at that!

The first lesson, unfortunately, was maths – *double* maths – with Miss Figgis. Miss Figgis had ears like a fruit bat, great sticking-out things that picked up the merest whisper. Lily, bursting with impatience, couldn't resist scribbling a note – **SOMETHING TO TELL YOU!!!** – and passing it across to Tara.

Tara glanced at it and raised her eyebrows. 'What?'

Lily shook her head. She pointed at Geraldine in the front row, industriously bent over her maths book.

Tara pulled a face: they both knew that Geraldine regarded note-passing as infantile. They were twelve-year-olds, after all, not babies. But this, thought Lily, was important. The only real piece of news she had ever had!

She watched as the note slowly made its way, via Meg Peters and Janice Turner, to the front of the class. Carefully, keeping one eye on Miss Figgis, Janice dropped it on Geraldine's desk. Geraldine looked round, annoyed. She caught Tara's eye and fixed her for a moment with a hard stare. She then, with the utmost disdain, as if it were something unwholesome, picked up the note between finger and thumb and deposited it on the floor.

Janice snorted and clapped a hand over her mouth.

Miss Figgis was on her in an instant. 'Something amuses you, Janice? Quadratic equations? You see the humour in them?'

Janice said, 'Sorry, Miss Figgis! Swallowed the wrong way.'

Geraldine rolled her eyes but reached out with a foot and shuffled the incriminating note safely out of sight beneath her desk.

The lesson continued, drearily – because there really *wasn't* anything amusing in quadratic equations, especially when you had an exciting tale to relate – until by breaktime even Tara was bursting with impatience.

'So what is it? What is it?'

'Not here.' Lily gave her a little push. 'Wait till we're outside!'

'What's the rush?' demanded Geraldine, but Lily and Tara had already gone, racing across the playing field to their favourite spot on the edge of the woods, where not many people went.

'*Now*,' said Tara. 'Tell!'

'Tell what?' said Geraldine.

'You wouldn't have to ask if you'd bothered to read the note!'

Crossly Geraldine said, 'I don't *read* notes! You shouldn't be passing them. Especially not in maths. You know what Miss Figgis said! She s—'

'Yeah, yeah! She said this was the Fifties and did I really want to grow up to be one of those silly little fluffy creatures who claimed maths was too difficult for their poor little brains?'

'Well, *do* you?' said Geraldine.

'Doesn't bother me,' said Tara. 'I've got fingers! I can count.'

Geraldine made an impatient scoffing sound.

'*Anyway*,' said Lily.

Tara said, 'Yes, anyway! What is it? I hope it's something exciting!'

'It's more a kind of . . . mystery,' said Lily.

Tara squealed loudly and delightedly. 'I love mysteries!'

Geraldine raised her eyes to heaven. She was always very superior, was Geraldine. 'Go on, then,' she said. 'Tell us, whatever it is!'

'*Well.*' Lily took a breath. 'It was this girl . . . I was on my way to school when she just suddenly appeared! Just jumped out of nowhere. Literally! You know?'

Tara nodded encouragement. Geraldine said, '*Literally?*'

'Yes!'

'Out of thin air?'

'Yes!'

Geraldine opened her mouth. 'People d—'

'Oh, just be quiet!' said Tara. 'I want to hear what happened!'

'Well, nothing,' said Lily. 'That's what's so odd! She just stood there, staring at me, and then she asked if I was Lily O'Grady, and I said I was, and she seemed kind of puzzled, like I didn't look how she expected me to look, and then she said, "*Oh, rats!*"'

'Rats?' said Geraldine.

'Rats!'

'You mean, like she'd made some kind of mistake?'

'Yes! She seemed quite cross about it.'

Geraldine nodded. 'Obviously got the wrong Lily O'Grady.'

'But . . .' Lily faltered. 'How many Lily O'Gradys could there be?'

'Loads, probably. If you look in the telephone book, I'll bet there's dozens.'

'But I'm not in the telephone book!'

'I know *you're* not. I'm just pointing out that Lily O'Grady is quite a common name. Not like Jasmine Appleblossom, or Gertrude Witherspoon, or—'

'Who's Jasmine Appleblossom?' said Tara.

'Nobody! I'm just giving you an example.'

'Oh. So is that it, then?'

'No!' Lily said it rather desperately. She obviously hadn't told the story properly. 'She was weird. You know? Like, *seriously* weird. Her hair was bright yellow, all sticking up in spikes like a dandelion!' She demonstrated, plucking at her own hair (black, cut short, with a fringe). 'It looked absolutely ridiculous! *And* the way she was dressed! Pukey purple tights with orange splodges. She'd even painted her lips to go with them! Puke purple, same as her tights. Honestly, it was really creepy! She just sprang up out of nowhere.'

Geraldine, very kindly and gently, said, 'She might have *seemed* to spring up out of nowhere, but actually people don't.'

'Well, *she* did!' said Lily. 'And then she said, "Try again!" and vanished.'

'Back into thin air.'

'*Yes.*'

'You mean, you didn't see where she went.'

'Because I told you . . . she just disappeared! One minute she was there; the next minute she wasn't. I just don't see where she could have come from!'

'*Where* did you say you were,' said Tara, 'when she jumped out at you? Where exactly were you?'

'I'd just got to the corner of Barclay Road.'

'Isn't that where that Spotlight place is?'

'Spotlight Academy?'

'The drama school. I bet that's where she came from! They're real show-offs, that lot. Sort that *would* paint their lips purple and go around looking like dandelions. There were some at the bus stop the other day, all shrieking and flapping about in their stupid red cloaks. Stuck out like sore plums!'

'Or thumbs,' said Geraldine.

'Whatever!' Tara waved a hand. 'Probably on her way in and suddenly saw you and thought you were someone else. That's why she said rats, cos she realised she'd got it wrong.'

'But how did she know my name?' Lily wasn't yet ready to give in. The mystery couldn't be solved as easily as that! 'Even if there *are* lots of other Lily O'Gradys, how did she know that I was one?'

'Maybe cos she lives in your road?'

'I've never seen her! I'd jolly well notice something like that,' said Lily. 'And where did she *come* from? Springing out like that! It was just so weird.'

'I'll tell you what else is weird,' said Geraldine. 'Don't turn round, but there's a boy over there, looking at you.'

'A boy?' said Lily. 'Looking at *me*?'

'Well, don't make it *obvious*,' said Geraldine.

CHAPTER 2

Her words came too late – Lily had already spun round. The boy stood at the edge of the woods, on the other side of the wire netting. He had curly black hair and the bluest eyes she had ever seen – and he was, quite unmistakably, looking at Lily. She felt her cheeks grow pink. Boys never looked at Lily! They looked at Geraldine, so cool and classy, with her bright red-gold hair that hung halfway down her back (demurely tied in plaits for school). They looked at chunky freckle-faced Tara, with her wide cheeky grin. They didn't look at Lily. Lily was just – well, Lily! Small and insignificant, like a little ant, buzzing about the place (as someone had once kindly informed her). What sort of boy would look at an ant?

'Can we help you?' said Geraldine. She didn't say it in a particularly friendly fashion. More like, *What do you think you're doing, staring at us?* The boy's cheeks fired up. Lily felt for him; she knew what it was like to be embarrassed.

'S-sorry!' He took a step backwards. 'I was looking for my gr—' He hesitated. He seemed reluctant to take his eyes off Lily. 'I was looking for my great-grandmother!'

Tara giggled. 'Great-grandmother?'

His cheeks, at that, grew even redder.

'Do I take it you've lost her?' said Geraldine.

He mumbled something which might have been yes, said again that he was sorry, shot one last apologetic glance at Lily and disappeared into the woods. They stood, watching him go.

'Well!' Tara giggled again. 'That's a first . . . being mistaken for somebody's grandmother!'

'*Great*-grandmother,' said Geraldine.

It was Lily's cheeks now that were starting to burn.

She felt hurt and indignant. How could he have taken her for his great-grandmother? Just because he'd been looking at Lily didn't have to mean he'd thought she was an old lady. He might just have been looking at her because – *well*. Just because. Because she had a cute little face! Her dad always said she had a cute little face. It wasn't absolutely impossible that someone might find her worth looking at.

'Shame, really,' said Tara.

'Why?' said Lily. 'Why is it a shame?' She said it rather fiercely.

Tara went off into peals of happy laughter. 'Thought for a moment he might have fancied you!'

Even Geraldine permitted herself a little smirk, before quickly assuring Lily that of course she didn't actually *look* like a great-grandmother.

'Not even a grandmother! But you can see why he might have thought it . . . I mean, at first glance. From a distance. If the sun was in his eyes, or – or he just caught a glimpse of you. I mean, you are so *tiny*, and if she's one of those little old ladies that's all wizened and shrunk . . . I mean, it's sort of understandable.'

Tara (who had ambitions of becoming an actress) immediately bent double and began tottering forward as if using a walking frame. Lily could see that it was going to be a big joke between the two of them. This boy who had thought Lily was his great-grandmother! What a hoot!

'To be serious for a minute,' said Geraldine, 'I suppose it's always possible if she's really that ancient she might sometimes go wandering off.'

'So then they'd have to send him out to find her and he'd end up taking Lily back with him . . . *Look, Mum, I got her!*'

'His mum might not even notice,' said Geraldine. 'Not if she's shrunk to the size of a doll!'

'You've got to admit,' said Tara, abandoning her walking frame, 'it's pretty funny. You have to laugh!' She gave Lily a playful poke.

Lily forced herself to smile.

'Those eyes,' said Tara. She did a mock swoon. 'I could go for him, no problem!'

Yes, but he wasn't looking at you, thought Lily. *He was looking at ME*. Who was to say he hadn't suddenly caught sight of her and been captivated by her cute face? It could happen! Just because it never had didn't mean it never *could*.

Tara gave a little skip. 'Talking of boys—'

'Didn't know we were,' said Geraldine.

'I was just going to *say* –' Tara did another skip – 'next Saturday me and Derek are going to the Festival of Britain . . . just us, by ourselves! Our mums said we could. They said we're old enough. I'm really looking forward to it! Mum says she wouldn't let me go with just anybody, but she never worries when I'm with Derek. She says he's got enough common sense for the two of us!'

'And, of course –' Geraldine said it slyly – 'he's not your boyfriend.'

Tara gave an impish grin. She always hotly denied that

Derek – the famous Derek, that no one had ever met – was anything other than 'just a boy who happens to live next door'. But he was, undeniably, a boy. And Geraldine sometimes went to the pictures with her cousin, who was also a boy, and, moreover, had friends who were boys. Geraldine had actually been introduced to them. All Lily had was Thomas, who was her brother and ten years old and thus far too young to be of any use. Who wanted to be introduced to a pack of ten-year-olds who still thought it fun to run around the back garden with water pistols?

'I'll tell you what,' said Geraldine, 'the thing you simply *must* go on is the Rotor!'

Tara squealed and said, '*Yesss!*'

'What's the Rotor?' said Lily.

It sounded like something that might be used on a farm. Would they have a farming section at the Festival of Britain? She supposed they might. Miss Carpenter had impressed upon them that the festival was intended 'to celebrate some of our country's greatest achievements

. . . something to be proud of!' She had said that if they went – 'Which I very much hope you will' – they would see exhibitions of everything under the sun. The sea, the sky, the polar regions . . . There was even, she said, a twelve-ton steam engine. The steam engine seemed particularly to have impressed her. 'Imagine, girls! Twelve tons! Truly an industrial wonder.' Maybe, thought Lily, that was what the Rotor was. Hopefully, she said, 'Is it the twelve-ton steam engine?'

'No!' Tara gave a hoot of laughter. 'It's this huge great revolving drum that you step down into and it just keeps going round and round until in the end the floor drops away and—'

'The *floor* drops away?' said Lily, alarmed.

'Yes, but by then you're stuck to the side, so it's all right, you couldn't move even if you wanted to.'

'What, and it's still going round?'

'Yes, it never stops.'

Lily gave a squeak. 'Don't you get giddy?'

'No! It's so slow you hardly notice.'

'I'd be sick!'

'Oh, well, you,' said Tara. 'Not normal people!'

'So how do you get stuck to the side?'

'We did it in science,' said Geraldine. 'If you'd been listening!'

'I do listen,' said Lily. 'It's just that I don't always remember.'

Geraldine tutted, impatiently. 'Centrifugal force?'

There was a pause; then Tara nodded, knowingly. 'Centrifungal force.'

'*Fugal*,' snapped Geraldine. 'Centri*fugal*!'

'Whatever!' Tara dismissed it, airily. 'Fungal, fugal . . . what's the difference? They still get stuck to the sides.'

Geraldine, considerably irritated, opened her mouth, but Tara had already gone prancing ahead, chanting loudly, for all to hear:

'Lily's got an ad*mirer*, Lily's got an ad*mirer*!'

Lily shoved at her. 'Stop it!'

Tara cackled rather wildly. 'Don't you wish he was?'

'Not really,' said Lily. She crossed her fingers behind

her back. It had to be quite one of the biggest lies she had ever told.

Tara cackled again. 'But blue eyes!' she said.

They really had been the brightest blue that Lily had ever seen. The memory of them almost entirely banished any thoughts of the mysterious girl with the dandelion haircut. Imagine if the blue-eyed boy really *had* been looking at her because he thought she was cute! Imagine if he were her boyfriend and they went to the Festival of Britain together, and imagine if they went on the weird Rotor thing and maybe, after all, she wouldn't get sick, though perhaps she might be just a little nervous, what with the floor falling away, so that he would take her hand and hold it very tightly, and that's how they would be when they got stuck to the side, going round and round, still holding hands, and everyone would smile and say how sweet they looked . . .

All through history with Mrs Dewey she dreamt that the blue-eyed boy was holding her hand. All through

English with Miss Carpenter, too, even though English was one of Lily's favourite subjects and Miss Carpenter one of her favourite teachers and they were reading *Jane Eyre*, which was one of her favourite books. She wasn't sure she ought to be letting any boy, blue-eyed or not, intrude on *Jane Eyre*. There was nothing terribly wrong *as such*, Miss Carpenter had once said, with heavy emphasis, in letting oneself indulge in love's young dream.

'So long as you take care not to become obsessed. Remember, girls, this is 1951 . . . the possibilities are endless. Aim high, cast off your fetters! You can be whatever you choose to be. All doors are open! Seize the day! Just *do not become obsessed*.'

Lily wondered uncomfortably, as she lost her place in *Jane Eyre* and realised she was on totally the wrong page, whether daydreaming in class could be counted as obsession. She honestly didn't want to be someone who had boys on the brain, but his eyes had been so *very* blue! Even Tara had swooned. And for those first few dizzying moments, before he had ruined it by talking about his great-grandmother, she had actually allowed herself to believe he might be looking at her the way boys looked at Geraldine and Tara.

Of course, she knew that most probably, as Geraldine had suggested, it was simply that the sun had been in his eyes and all he had been able to make out was this tiny little matchstick figure standing on the wrong side of the wire netting. Geraldine was always so sensible! And she was almost always right. He had seen what had looked from a distance as if it could be his great-grandmother; all the rest, thought Lily, sadly, was just her imagination. And now she had gone and missed a whole page of *Jane Eyre*! Miss Carpenter would be disappointed in her. One of her best pupils wasting her time in idle daydreams! Tonight, vowed Lily, she would not only read the page she had missed, she would read the whole of the following chapter. And she wouldn't let her hand be held once!

*

'Now, don't forget,' urged Tara, as they parted company at the school gates at ten to four, 'have a look down Barclay Road . . . I bet you'll see loads of kids coming out of that Spotlight place. If you keep your eyes peeled, you might even see *her*!'

Lily did have just a quick glance. A group of Spotlight girls were actually coming towards her, swinging their bags and chattering, but Dandelion Head definitely wasn't amongst them. Lily didn't need to keep her eyes peeled; there was nobody even remotely like her. They all looked perfectly normal, apart from their bright red cloaks (which Lily secretly admired). Nobody had spiky hair or was wearing purple tights. They weren't even shrieking or showing off. Maybe talking a bit loudly, and taking up rather a lot of the pavement (which Miss Carpenter would have had something to say about), but there wasn't anyone mad or weird like Dandelion Head. In any case, even if she *had* been one of them, it still wouldn't explain how she could have appeared out of thin air. Because she *had* appeared out of thin air – no matter what Geraldine might say. Geraldine didn't know everything, in spite of coming top of exams and being so frighteningly clever. It remained, thought Lily, a total mystery.

The next day, Lily said to Tara, 'I had a look at that Spotlight place. There was a whole crowd of girls coming out, but I didn't see *her*.'

'Did you talk to them?' said Tara.

'Talk to them? No! Was I supposed to?'

'You could at least have asked them.'

'Asked them what?' said Lily, bewildered.

'If they knew her!'

'Oh. It didn't occur to me . . . You never said anything about asking them!'

'Oh, really!' Tara made an impatient tutting sound. 'All you had to do was say, "Excuse me, do you happen to know a girl that looks like a dandelion and wears purple tights?"'

'And then what?'

'We'd know if she was one of them!'

'Or not,' added Geraldine.

In resentful tones Lily said, 'Even if she was, it still wouldn't explain anything! I looked and looked and there wasn't *anywhere* she could have hidden herself.'

Tara, plainly not convinced, said, 'Hmph!'

'I'm telling you!' said Lily. Why wouldn't anyone believe her?

Tara shook her head in wonderment. 'Not even *asking*.'

'You didn't *say* to ask! You didn't—'

'Before we get all aerated,' said Geraldine, 'there is one possible explanation.'

'What?'

'It could all have been in the mind.'

Lily was indignant. 'Are you saying I made it up?'

'No! I'm just saying it could have been in the mind.'

'Like a pigment,' said Tara.

There was a pause. Lily giggled in spite of herself.

'Like a *what*?' said Geraldine.

'A pigment! Pigment of the imagination. It's what it's called,' said Tara, obviously proud to have found a word that Geraldine didn't know. 'When your mind plays tricks . . . they call it a pigment. Dunno why. But that's what they call it. Pigment of the imagination.'

'Might be what you call it,' said Geraldine. 'Some of us refer to it as a figment.'

'Whatever!' Tara waved a hand. 'There is only one way,' she informed Lily, 'to tell whether something's real or whether it's just a pigment. Poke it with a finger! If it's solid, it's real; if not, it's a pigment.'

'Excuse *me*,' said Lily, 'Dandelion Head is not a pigment! *Figment*.' She corrected herself hastily before Geraldine could start on her eye-rolling. 'I didn't imagine it!'

'No, but if it happens again,' insisted Tara, 'you know what to do . . . just poke her and see!'

CHAPTER
3

For a while Lily dutifully stopped to have a quick look down Barclay Road on her way to and from school every day, but Dandelion Head never reappeared. She wasn't brave enough to ask any of the Spotlight crowd whether they knew a girl with bright yellow hair and purple tights. It sounded so silly! Tara, growing impatient, said, 'I'll come and do it if you're too scared!' But she didn't want Tara doing it. Geraldine, maybe, but Geraldine didn't offer. Tara was obviously longing to! Lily could just see her strutting up, all full of herself, dragging Lily in her wake, making them both look ridiculous. It would be like, *you needn't think you're anyone special just because you go to drama school!*

'I've got an idea,' said Tara. 'Why don't I go and talk to them while you hide behind a tree and pretend you're not there?'

'I told you,' snapped Lily, 'there aren't any trees!'

Certainly not any big enough to hide behind.

'Hmm . . . really makes you wonder if she *was* just a pigment,' said Geraldine. She glanced slyly at Lily, obviously expecting her to giggle again, but Lily humped a shoulder, refusing to laugh at the same joke twice. Pigment, figment, it simply wasn't funny. She knew what she had seen! Why couldn't they believe her?

As the months, and then even a whole year, came and went without any sign of Dandelion Head, Lily reluctantly began to accept that it was a mystery which might never be solved. She still didn't accept that she had been imagining things. She *had* seen the girl and the girl *had* known her name and she *had* sprung up out of nowhere. But life moved on, and even Tara, in the end, found other subjects to occupy her. She had gone to the Festival of Britain with Derek and been on the Rotor and for a while couldn't stop talking about it. She and Derek had won the junior table-tennis tournament at their local youth club and she was seriously thinking of becoming a professional table-tennis player. She and Derek had been to the cinema and seen *Lassie Come Home*.

'And *still* you claim he's not your boyfriend? Sounds like one to me,' said Geraldine. And then to Lily she muttered, 'I shall scream if she doesn't stop going on about him!'

Lily supposed that it was a bit tiresome, but anything was better, she thought, than constantly being nagged at to do things you didn't want to do. She didn't actually forget about Dandelion Head, but she no longer braced herself as she approached Barclay Road every morning, nor stopped to peer down it every afternoon. All she ever saw was the Spotlight crew in their dashing scarlet cloaks.

In any case, other things were happening in her life. Queen Elizabeth II had been crowned and they had all had a day off school. Mum and Dad had bought a television set specially so they could watch; some of the neighbours had even come in. And then of course there had been the Festival of Britain. Lily had gone with Mum and Thomas, and had marvelled at the Dome of Discovery and the Skylon towering in the air. Thomas had wanted to go on the Rotor, boasting that *he* wouldn't be scared when the floor fell away and they all found themselves stuck to the side. Lily hadn't been so sure, but Tara would be bound to ask whether she had been on it, and would jeer at her for being a coward if she admitted that she hadn't, so down they had stepped into the revolving drum, her and Thomas, with Mum watching, because Mum could afford to be a coward, and, after all, as it turned out, it hadn't been so very frightening, nothing like the big dipper at the seaside, when she had screamed and squeezed her eyes tight shut and clutched so hard at the metal bar which locked them in that Dad had had to prise her fingers open when they finally came back to earth.

Lily wasn't, she thought sadly, a very brave sort of person. She saw herself, in her daydreams, on the big dipper with the blue-eyed boy. He wouldn't mind that she wasn't brave! He would put his arm round her and hold her tight. Sometimes she even dared let herself imagine him giving a little fond laugh and kissing her, though she tried not to let the dream go too far if other people were around, like if she was in class or walking to school, because it made her cheeks grow all hot and pink.

She knew Miss Carpenter wouldn't approve. Miss Carpenter would say she was in danger of becoming obsessed. But her dreamworld was such a comfort! And the blue-eyed boy *had* been looking at her. Try as she might, she couldn't stop thinking of him. Not all the time, of course – just now and again. Like, for instance, when they went to visit Auntie Marjorie and Uncle Gavin one Sunday afternoon. Even Mum had to admit that visiting Auntie Marjorie and Uncle Gavin was a bit of a trial, even though Auntie Marjorie was her sister.

'We just have to bear with it,' said Mum.

The Little Angel was what they had to bear with. The Little Angel was ten years old and was called Melanie, fondly referred to by Auntie Marjorie as Mel, or even, sometimes, Mellie, which was just asking for trouble if you stopped to think about it. Mum, try as she might, found it difficult to be cross with Thomas gleefully chanting 'Smelly Mellie, Smelly Mellie,' as they waited at the corner of Barclay Road for the bus to Glendale Avenue. (Lily had one quick peek down the road, just in case, but on a Sunday afternoon not even the Spotlight crowd were there.)

'Smelly Mellie, Smelly Mellie,' chanted Thomas, as they arrived at Glendale Avenue with its little cluster of gnomes in the front garden.

'Thomas, that's enough!' said Mum. 'And don't kick the garden gnomes!'

'I'd take a hammer to them if I had my way,' growled Dad.

Lily could never understand why Dad was so set

against the garden gnomes. She had pleaded for them to have some in their own garden, but Dad had said 'over my dead body'. What was his objection?

After they had all trooped indoors and been treated to the sight of the Little Angel performing its latest party piece – 'On the Good Ship Lollipop', yuck, yuck, yuck! – with Mum politely applauding and Dad having to shove Thomas's head under his arm to stop the rude noises that were coming from him, they were all taken into the front room and sat down for tea – always the best part of the visit. Thomas, as usual, had to be physically restrained from helping himself to cake before he had eaten any of Auntie Marjorie's fish-paste sandwiches, which he should have known by now were something that just had to be got through before you came to the good bit. He really didn't have any manners at all, thought Lily, but then the Little Angel hardly had any either. Halfway through the meal – before they had even got as far as the cake – there was a ring at the door and the Little Angel went scampering off to answer it. She reappeared, briefly, to announce that 'That was Barry. We're going up the park,' and went rushing off. Didn't even ask permission, just said, 'All right?' and was off.

Auntie Marjorie shook her head. 'Her boyfriend.' She pulled a comical face. 'They're inseparable! One of our neighbours said she saw them the other day walking along the High Street holding hands. She said it was just so sweet!'

'There is something rather touching about it when they're that young and innocent,' agreed Mum. 'It's like little Maisie up the road. You know Maisie?' She turned to Lily. Lily nodded, glumly. 'She's got a boyfriend now! She's around the same age as Melanie, and he can't be very much older . . . You see them wandering about with their arms round each other, totally lost to the world!'

'Isn't ten a bit young?' said Dad.

'Not these days,' Auntie Marjorie assured him.

'Even this one –' Mum gave Thomas a playful poke – 'even he's got a little girlfriend! Oh yes, you have,' she said, as Thomas protested. 'Don't deny it! You've been seen!'

'Oh, they're all at it now,' said Uncle Gavin. 'How about Lily? I'll bet she's not behindhand!'

Lily felt her cheeks turn a painful red.

'Come on, then,' said Uncle Gavin. 'Don't be shy!'

'You leave her be,' said Dad. 'She'll have a boyfriend when she's good and ready. Won't you? Mmm?' He gave her a reassuring hug. 'Why be in such a rush to grow up? I was almost sixteen before I dared even speak to a girl!'

Lily could only be thankful that the Little Angel hadn't still been there to witness her moment of shame. How her lip would have curled!

CHAPTER
4

The following week, they broke for the summer holidays. Lily wandered happily home in the sunshine. She was having a particularly beautiful dream in which Auntie Marjorie and Uncle Gavin, together with the Little Angel, had come to visit. They were all sitting down eating tea when there was a ring at the door, and it was him, the boy with the blue eyes, come to ask if she would care to go for a walk. She saw herself racing back to tell Mum. She saw Mum smiling indulgently – 'Her boyfriend! They're inseparable' – and the Little Angel's mouth dropping open in disbelief.

She had just reached one of the best parts, with Mum saying how a neighbour had seen them holding hands – 'She thought it just the sweetest thing!' – when all of a sudden, *whoosh!* From out of nowhere Dandelion Head appeared.

'*You,*' said Lily.

'Me,' said Dandelion Head. And then, subjecting Lily to a prolonged and irritable gaze, she threw up her hands and cried, 'I can't believe it! I've gone and done it again!'

'Done what?' said Lily.

'Got the date wrong!' She said it impatiently, as if Lily should have known. 'What *is* it?'

'The date?'

'Yes! What is it?'

'It's the fifteenth of July,' said Lily.

'Yes, but what year?'

She was asking her what *year* it was?

'Tell me!'

Stolidly, Lily said, '1953.'

'Oh, rats! Rats, rats, rats!' She stamped a foot. 'Still too early!'

There was a pause. *I am not going to ask her too early for what*, thought Lily. *She is obviously quite dotty, and I have humoured her long enough.*

'1953 . . . that rings bells! It's when Elizabeth the Second gets crowned, isn't it?'

'She's already been crowned,' said Lily.

'*Really?*'

'Yes, really.' What planet was this girl living on? You couldn't forget the coronation!

Dandelion Head pulled a face. 'History's never been one of my best subjects.'

It was hardly history, thought Lily. It might be in a few years' time, but it wasn't history *now*. Not proper historical history. She began to think that maybe this girl had some kind of problem. Unless – a rather frightening thought – it was Lily who had a problem? Was she dreaming? She remembered, belatedly, what Tara had said: if you want to find out whether someone's real or just a pigment, try poking them with your finger. Cautiously, Lily stretched out a hand and prepared to poke.

'What are you doing?' screeched Dandelion Head. She careered backwards into the path of a woman who was passing by.

'Do you mind?' snapped the woman. 'Honestly! Young people today have no manners!'

'Now see what you made me do,' grumbled Dandelion Head.

Lily swallowed. Either she really was dreaming or Dandelion Head was real. Solid at any rate. The poor woman had almost been sent flying across the pavement. No wonder she had been so cross! How, in any case, would a girl wearing hideous purple tights manage to worm her way into Lily's private dreamworld? And why, for that matter, was she still wearing exactly the same stupid clothes she had been wearing before? Did she never change them? Maybe, thought Lily, it was some kind of weird school uniform.

'You don't go to the Spotlight Academy, do you?' she said.

Not that she had ever seen any of the girls from

Spotlight wearing purple tights, or, at any rate, not ones with orange swirls.

'What,' said Dandelion Head, 'is the Spotlight Academy?' And then, as Lily opened her mouth to explain: 'Don't bother – it's not important. This really is *too* much! You'd never believe the risks I run, coming here. I have to do things in such a tearing hurry; it's no wonder I keep messing up!' She glared accusingly at Lily, as if it were her fault. 'It's nowhere near as easy as you might think! It's not just a case of punching in numbers; there's a lot more to it than that. And if you're having to look over your shoulder all the time, in case someone comes in and catches you at it . . . well, it's surprising I even managed to get the right *place*. Not to mention,' she added, 'the right person!'

'I'm sorry,' said Lily. 'I haven't the foggiest idea what you're talking about.'

'No, well.' Dandelion Head heaved an impatient sigh. 'You couldn't really be expected to. You're still very primitive.'

'Excuse me,' said Lily, indignantly. Who was she calling primitive? 'My mum and dad,' she informed Dandelion, 'have a television set! *And* a fridge.' They didn't have a washing machine yet, but someone in their road did. Mum had been to see it. She had said it was a marvel.

Dandelion Head gave a little laugh. Quite a kindly little laugh, but a laugh all the same.

Lily felt hurt. Mum and Dad had been so proud when the television set had been installed! There were only two other families they knew that had one. Even the fridge was what Dad called *cutting-edge technology*. Lots of people still had to make do with keeping milk and butter in a cool place and hoping they didn't go off.

'Tell me,' said Dandelion Head. 'Your television set . . . it's still just black and white, I guess?'

Defensively, Lily said, 'Everybody's is black and white! *Pictures* are in colour.'

'Pictures?' Dandelion Head seemed puzzled. 'What pictures? You mean, paintings?'

'Films! *Talkies.*'

'Oh!' She laughed again. 'So you've finally got them!'

'Talkies have been around for *years*,' said Lily. Why was she even bothering to engage in this mad conversation? Dandelion Head was obviously loopy. Obviously playing some silly sort of game. 'For your information –' Lily couldn't resist a bit of boasting – 'we've got a telephone as well as a TV. What is more,' she added, 'it's our own. We don't have to share it.'

'People share *telephones*?' said Dandelion Head. She plainly found it difficult to believe.

'Sometimes they do,' said Lily. 'They call it a party line.' Geraldine's parents had a party line – which must, thought Lily, be very inconvenient. Geraldine had told them that every now and again, when you picked up the receiver to make a call, you could hear the other people talking. That is, the people you shared with. So then you had to put the receiver back and wait till they hung up. It was bad manners, said Geraldine, to listen in on other people's conversations. 'You must have heard of party lines?' said Lily.

Dandelion shook her head. 'Can't say I have, but I can hardly be expected to remember every last little detail! I know you don't have mobiles. *They* don't come in till –' she waved a hand – 'much later. And you certainly don't have the internet! I know that. Don't even have computers. Not generally. I suppose a few people might, in offices. Not for personal use. That doesn't happen for ages.' She stopped and looked searchingly at Lily. 'You still don't know what I'm talking about, do you?'

That was because she was talking rubbish, thought Lily. 'Are you *sure* you don't go to Spotlight?' she said.

'*I do not go to Spotlight.* How many more times?'

'I thought perhaps you might be doing one of those improvisation things.' Tara had told them about improvisations, or improverisations, as she called them. 'They act out these little scenarios. Make them up as they go.'

It was the only explanation. Either that, or Dandelion Head really was completely batty.

'I'll tell you what,' said Dandelion, 'I've got a few minutes. Let's go over to that seat and talk, instead of just standing about.'

Lily, not being at all sure that she wanted to talk, pointed out that the seat Dandelion was heading for wasn't intended for just anyone; it was meant to be for people that were waiting for their buses to arrive, but Dandelion, tossing her head, said a seat was a seat and there wasn't anyone else using it, so what was Lily's problem? Reluctantly, Lily trailed after her.

Dandelion Head, in businesslike tones, said, 'Right. Okay — that is the correct usage, isn't it? *Okay?*'

'I suppose so,' said Lily.

'I mean, it's current? Yes? I'm actually pretty good at languages. In fact —' Dandelion Head nodded, obviously pleased with herself — 'twentieth-century dialect is one of my special subjects. If you want to become an observer and make little trips back in time, you have to have the lingo. Well, obviously!' She gave a cackle. 'Be a bit stupid if I arrived in the middle of the twentieth century saying "gadzooks" and "forsooth" . . . I'd soon be sussed out! Is that the right expression? "Sussed out"? Do you say that? No! I can see that you don't. It is in use, I can assure you! I got ninety per cent in my last linguistics test. *Unlike* history . . . I only got fifty-four in that! But that's all right; I don't aim to be a historian. Too dry for my liking. All that boring research! Simple time travel will do me.'

Lily, listening in complete bewilderment, shot a nervous glance over her shoulder. Dandelion Head might have *seemed* solid – well, she presumably must be, or she wouldn't have sent that poor woman flying. But suppose it was all just happening in Lily's imagination and neither Dandelion Head nor the woman really existed? Geraldine could be right! It could all be in the mind. For all Lily knew she could be sitting there in the bus shelter all by herself, nodding and pulling faces at nothing.

'So!' Dandelion Head rapped Lily smartly on the hand. Lily jumped. 'Are you paying attention?'

'Yes!' Definitely solid. 'I'm listening!'

'So what did I just say?'

'You said . . . you said . . .'

'I said,' said Dandelion, 'that simple time travel would do me. Which means what, do you think?'

'Don't know,' said Lily.

'It means,' said Dandelion, obviously trying very hard to be patient, 'that I am from a different time. It means that you're the here and now, and I'm –' she made a circular motion with her hand, encouraging Lily to speak up – 'I'm . . .?'

'Dunno,' said Lily.

'It means I'm from the future. Yes? The future?'

'If you say so,' said Lily. Sometimes you just had to humour people.

Dandelion clicked her tongue. 'You are *familiar* with the idea of time travel, I suppose?'

'You mean, like in science fiction?'

'Like H. G. Wells. Don't tell me you've never read H. G. Wells?'

Lily brightened. '*War of the Worlds!*' At least it was

something she'd heard of. It was true she hadn't actually read it, because it wasn't the sort of book she generally went for. She preferred stories about school and ponies, like *No Peace for the Prefects* and *Jill's Gymkhana*. She didn't like to say so, though, in case Dandelion Head went all Geraldine on her and started casting her eyes heavenwards.

'Thing about H. G. Wells,' said Dandelion, 'he got a lot of stuff right. *He* knew about time travel! Don't dismiss it as fiction, when you've obviously never read it, like you've never heard the expression "sussed out", which I can assure you is perfectly valid! I expect languages just aren't your subject.'

Lily bristled. 'They are *so*!' She had almost come top of English last term. She would have done if Geraldine hadn't beaten her to it. But you couldn't really count Geraldine; she came top of everything.

'Simply because I haven't heard of "sussed out",' said Lily. 'I mean, it sounds like slang. We're not allowed to use slang!'

'Hmm!'

'Well, we're not! Miss Carpenter s—'

'Hang about!' Dandelion snatched a quick glance at her wrist. (What was she looking at? There wasn't anything there.) 'Thought so.' She started up. 'Gotta go! There was something I wanted to ask you, but I can't risk being caught. Don't worry, stay there – I'll be right back!'

Dandelion flapped a hand. Lily watched as she merged with a group of people that had just got off a bus. One minute she was there in their midst; the next, there was no sign of her. She must have turned the corner into Barclay Road. It was difficult to see where else she could have gone. Unless, once again, she had simply vanished into thin air.

CHAPTER
5

Lily supposed she might as well wait a few minutes. Not that she actually expected Dandelion Head to come back — not, at any rate, immediately. She had already got the date wrong twice! Well, if her story was to be believed, which obviously it wasn't. She obviously *did* go to the Spotlight Academy, whatever she said, and it had all been nothing but an exercise. One of Tara's *improverisations*. 'Get dressed up as if you're some kind of alien, then go out and tell people you're from the future and see how they react!' And then they would have been warned not to say they were at Spotlight because if they did that people would guess it was all just make-believe. Which it had to be, thought Lily. Just acting! Like that business of looking at her wrist, like she was looking at a watch, when there was nothing there to look at. All show!

It remained a bit of a mystery how Dandelion Head had known her name, and how she had suddenly arrived out of thin air. And what, for instance, was *her* name? Did she even have one? There were still bits that didn't make any sense. But then, coming from the future didn't make any sense either, no matter what H. G. Wells might have said.

Lily was about to give up and go home when she saw Dandelion Head striding towards her, a big grin on her face.

'Told you! Said I'd be back.' She nodded, complacently. 'I reckon I'm getting the hang of it . . . *Date – time – location.*' She checked them off on her fingers. 'First time we met, I got lucky! Could easily have arrived ten minutes too late and missed you entirely! It was just the year I got wrong.' She laughed. 'I'll be more careful in future! That's a joke,' she added. '*Future* . . . I *am* the future!'

'So what does that make me?' said Lily.

'You're the past!'

Lily wrestled with the idea. 'Yesterday was the past. Today's the present.'

'And tomorrow's the future! It's really quite simple if you stop to think about it. Anyway, I'm obviously getting the hang of things, so next time—'

'You're coming back *again*?' said Lily.

'You bet!' Dandelion gave one of her happy cackles of laughter. 'That's when the ball starts rolling!'

'What ball?'

'It's an *expression*,' said Dandelion.

'I know it's an expression! What's it supposed to mean?'

'It means I have to come back and check that everything's going according to plan. Make sure the timeline's holding.'

'What timeline?' Lily narrowed her eyes, suspiciously. 'I hope you don't think you're going to start meddling!'

'Just little tweaks. Goes on all the time.'

'What sort of little tweaks?'

'Don't worry – you won't even know it's happening! I've got it all planned.'

'I demand to know!' said Lily.

'Yeah, well, I'm sorry, I don't have time right now to take you through it. It's far too complicated; you'd never understand.'

'Try me!'

'Maybe when I come back. This is really just a flying visit. There's this thing I wanted to ask you. Not that it's that important, I'm just curious . . . Well, sit down, for goodness' sake! We can't talk standing up.'

They could just not talk at all, thought Lily. Resentfully, she perched herself on the edge of the seat. 'How do you know I'll still be here?'

'Why shouldn't you be here? I'll be back in a few months!'

'A lot can happen in a few months,' said Lily.

'My mum and dad might decide to move to Australia! Or anywhere. Then you wouldn't be able to find me!'

'Of course I'd be able to find you! So long as I put in the right details it doesn't matter which country you're in. Anyway, trust me! You're not going to move to Australia.'

Lily had to admit it wasn't very likely. 'But suppose I'm dead?'

'Why would you be dead?'

'People die,' said Lily. 'Girl at my school died. She got polio.' Brenda Ibbotson. It had been announced in morning prayers. Everyone had cried, even people who hadn't really known her.

'You're not going to get polio,' said Dandelion. 'And you're certainly not going to die!'

'How do you know I'm not going to die?'

'For goodness' sake, how many more times? Watch my lips: *I'm from the future!* I'd know if you were dead.

You're not dead! You'd think you'd be grateful. Just stop babbling – I don't have all day. There'd be an almighty row if anyone discovered what I was doing!'

'So why d—'

'Because! I'll explain another time. What I want to know, that day we first met—'

'Hardly call it *meeting*,' said Lily. 'Jumping out in front of someone and—'

'Yes, yes! I'm sorry! I didn't mean to startle you. I'd never done a solo trip before. I'm not at that level! Now, quick, just tell me . . . that first time, did anything else happen?'

'Like what?'

'Like, later on, did a boy come and talk to you?'

'How would I be expected to remember that? A *boy*, talking to me! Boys,' said Lily, not quite truthfully, in fact, not truthfully at all, 'are always talking to me.'

'Really?' Dandelion Head regarded her, doubtfully. 'Well, I think you might remember this one.' She tapped a finger on her wrist, then held out her wrist for Lily to see. Lily stared. Floating in mid-air was a picture – a photograph? – of the boy with blue eyes. How did she *do* that?

'Who is he?' said Lily. Was he at Spotlight as well? Come to think of it, he'd looked as if he might be an actor. Not just the blue eyes, but the clothes he had been wearing . . . a short red jacket and high-waisted black trousers like a Spanish dancer. Geraldine had remarked at the time that she didn't reckon he went to any of the local schools.

'Not a uniform *I've* ever seen.' Tara had agreed. 'Very snazzy, though!'

'So what did he say?' demanded Dandelion.

'Didn't really say anything very much,' said Lily.

'Huh! Just stared, I suppose, like a total ninny. I knew it!' Dandelion tapped again at her wrist and the picture disappeared. 'He obviously snuck in behind me. The cheek of it! I take all the risks and he gets a free trip. You wait till I see him!'

'But who is he?'

'It's a long story! I really don't have time right now. Gotta go or I'll be in trouble!'

'Oh, please,' begged Lily, 'please! Don't disappear without telling me who he is!'

CHAPTER
6

Too late. Dandelion Head had already gone. And who knew when she would be back, if ever? But Lily needed to know right now. Right this very minute! Who *was* the boy with the blue eyes, and why was Dandelion Head so cross with him?

They obviously knew each other. She bet they both went to Spotlight! All this talk about coming from the future . . . They'd probably been told to go out and talk to people and make up little stories, and Dandelion was resentful because Lily was the one *she* had picked and he had no right to interfere. Let him find someone of his own!

Lily felt better once she had worked it out. She knew

he couldn't have taken her for an old lady! It had just been him doing his acting. Making up a story. They must all have chosen different scenarios. Dandelion Head had decided to be from another planet – well, from another time. He had pretended to be searching for his great-grandmother. And it was Lily he had looked at! Not Tara, not Geraldine. *Lily.* It was all beginning to make sense!

It still didn't quite explain where Dandelion Head had got the photo from. Just produced it out of nowhere, like a rabbit out of a hat! Did they teach them conjuring tricks as well as acting? She supposed it was possible. If you were going to go on the stage, you would need all kinds of different skills. Acting, singing, dancing, fencing maybe? For being in Shakespeare? Horse riding. Acrobatics. Elocution. Conjuring tricks? It would no doubt come in extremely useful, knowing how to do conjuring tricks. Like if someone offered you a part as a magician, and you could say, oh, yes, I have a diploma in conjuring, and you would be able to show them how you could magic photographs out of nowhere.

Except there weren't any conjuring tricks, as far as Lily knew, that could make you magic *yourself* out of nowhere. Maybe on stage; not in real life. Doubts came flooding back. She *had* arrived out of nowhere! It wasn't all in Lily's head; she wasn't just a figment. She was solid! Except if that was the case – which it was, cos Lily had proved it – then where could she have come from?

'Do you think,' said Lily, later that evening, as they sat down to dinner, 'that there's such a thing as time travel?'

Dad said, 'Do little green men live on Mars?'

Whatever *that* had to do with anything.

'Dunno why they'd be green,' said Thomas. 'Just cos they're alien life forms. I mean, why's it always green? Why not orange or red or—'

'Sky-blue-pink!' Who cared? thought Lily. What did it matter *what* colour they were? 'I just want to know about people coming from the future!'

'Oh, that'll happen!' Thomas assured her of it, eagerly. 'Might even happen in our lifetimes.'

'You really think so?'

'Enough people have written books about it. Can't all be wrong.'

'You mean, people like H. G. Wells?'

'Now, there's a good writer,' said Dad. '*War of the Worlds* . . . A cracking tale!'

'Is it about time travel?'

'No, it's about aliens invading the Earth. Scary stuff!'

Mum frowned. Hastily, Dad said, 'All just fiction, of course.'

'But he got some things right! Didn't he?'

'Not time travel,' said Dad. 'That's an age-old dream! Just because they do it in comic strips doesn't mean it's going to happen.'

'For your information,' said Thomas, rather heatedly, 'it's not just in comic strips, it's in real books!'

'Still just fiction.'

'*Science* fiction. You do know,' said Thomas, 'why it's called *science* fiction?'

'No,' said Dad. 'Why is it called *science* fiction?'

'Cos it's based on real scientific possibilities. That's why!'

Lily looked at her brother with new respect. Scientific possibilities! This from the boy who had marched down the path at Glendale Avenue chanting 'Smellie Mellie' and kicking garden gnomes!

'Sooner or later,' said Thomas, 'what happens in science fiction happens in real life.'

'You mean, any minute now we're going to start blasting rockets into space?'

'Wanna bet?' said Thomas. 'Give it a couple of years, might even get as far as the moon. Might even get *men* up there.'

'Or even women,' suggested Mum.

Dad chuckled. 'That'll be the day! Men *or* women!'

'You wait,' said Thomas. 'You'll see!'

'But what about *time travel?*' said Lily. She did wish they would keep to the subject! She wasn't interested in men on the moon or rockets being blasted into space. She was interested in people coming back from the future. 'You really, honestly think it could happen?'

'You'd better believe it!' said Thomas. 'Somewhere in the world they're probably already working on it. Already conducting experiments . . . sending people into the future to have a look around!'

'What about sending them into the past?'

'Yeah, that would be pretty useful! Be able to see what had actually gone on, 'stead of just relying on history books. Course, they'd have to make sure they didn't interfere with the timeline, like deciding certain people could be wiped out . . . Hitler, for instance. And stuff like railway accidents and plagues.'

'But wouldn't that be a good thing?' said Lily. 'Imagine if they could come back and stop the Black Death!'

'Wouldn't be allowed. There'd have to be very strict rules. Like in this book I read.' Thomas's eyes gleamed, as he told them about it. '*Theory of Time Travel* by this man that's a professor . . . A *professor*,' said Thomas. He paused to let it sink in. 'Real professor, from America!

'Cording to him, they're almost there. Might even *be* there for all we know. Obviously, at the moment, they're still having to keep it hidden.'

'Obviously,' said Dad.

'Just until they've got it all worked out. Could take a while. He was saying, this professor, there'll have to be international agreements. Can't have one country going off and doing its own thing. He thinks probably what they'll do, they'll issue special licences. Make sure no one goes back and changes stuff. Just observe, that's all they'll be allowed to do. Cos just one tiny unimportant little change that you'd think wouldn't make any difference could alter the entire course of history!'

'You reckon?' said Dad.

'Stands to reason! Suppose, f'r instance, that party you went to, where you first met Mum and asked her to go out with you, suppose it didn't happen cos of someone messing with the timeline? You might both be married to other people and me and Lily wouldn't even be here!'

'A sobering thought,' said Dad.

'I wouldn't laugh if I was you. Could be people out there right now, messing with our lives.'

'I'm sure you're right,' said Dad.

'It's not just me,' said Thomas, earnestly. 'There are people that have studied these things. They don't just make stuff up out of nowhere. They know what they're talking about!'

Dad inclined his head. 'I bow to their superior knowledge. I await the arrival of space travel with bated breath.'

'But time travel,' urged Lily. 'That could already be here?'

'Absolutely!' said Thomas. 'You want to read the book – it's a real eye-opener! Things that go on without people realising . . . It's so top secret even governments don't always know!'

'Only the professor,' said Dad.

'Yes, cos he's looked into it! He has no doubt *whatsoever*,' said Thomas, 'that it's actually going on right under our noses. He says it might still only be at the experimental stage, but they've definitely proved they can do it!'

So it really was possible. It really could be happening right now! People from the future, materialising all over the place, suddenly appearing out of nowhere. It would certainly account for the way Dandelion Head had sprung out in front of her. *And* for the purple leggings and the yellow hair. They were probably the height of fashion where she came from. It could even explain how she had done that conjuring trick with the photograph. What it didn't explain was why she had picked on Lily, and, most important of all, it didn't explain who the boy was or why he had been looking for his great-grandmother. That, for Lily, was the real mystery.

She wondered, as she went to school on Monday, whether she would tell the others. If they hadn't believed her before, they certainly wouldn't believe her now. Even if she assured them that she had tried poking and that Dandelion Head was so solid she had sent a woman flying across the pavement. Geraldine would just say, in her boringly sensible way, that Lily had probably poked a bit too vigorously and overbalanced herself. In other words, that *she* had sent the woman flying. As for the idea of people coming back from the future, she could just imagine the pitying looks that would pass between the two of them.

Lily might plead that 'People have written books about it!', but Tara would only make one of her rude trumpeting noises and go, 'Yeah, comic books!' Even if Lily were to say '*Real* books' and tell them about the professor, Geraldine would only shake her head, rather sadly, as if Lily was a small child who still believed in fairies. She might be impressed though, if Lily explained that the reason science fiction was called science fiction was that it was based on real scientific possibilities. 'Sooner or later,' she would say, 'what happens in science fiction happens in real life!'

Geraldine would probably like the idea that somewhere

in the world – America, most likely, or Russia – they might already be conducting experiments, sending people into the future or back into the past. For someone with a scientific brain it might not seem so far-fetched. Geraldine was always saying that you had to be open to new ideas. Tara would jeer because Tara didn't have a scientific brain any more than Lily did. But Geraldine was clever! She knew about centrifuges and – and molecules and – and that thing they'd done only last week about stuff passing through semi-permeable membranes . . . osmosis! That was what it was called! Lily couldn't now remember what a semi-permeable membrane was, or what happened when stuff passed through it, but Geraldine would know! She might be quite eager to discuss the possibilities of time travel.

Perhaps, after all, thought Lily, she would take a chance and tell them. She waited till they were on their way across the field at breaktime, heading for their usual spot by the woods (where the blue-eyed boy had stood, staring at her).

'You'll never guess what happened,' she said. 'I s—'

It was as far as she got. Her words were cut short by Tara suddenly waving a hand and shrieking, 'Hey, Danny! Hope you enjoyed it, the other night!'

Lily and Geraldine exchanged glances. Since when did any of them address Daniela Sabatini as Danny? They weren't exactly friends! In the same year group maybe, but Daniela had her own little gang of admirers. She didn't hobnob with the likes of Lily and Tara, not even with Geraldine, for all that Geraldine was so smart. She did at least *acknowledge* Geraldine, but had never, as far as Lily could recall, even bothered to say more than half a dozen words to her and Tara. And here was Tara gaily calling out 'Hey, Danny!' as if they were best mates.

'She came to the youth club,' explained Tara. 'Came with this boy, Cameron.'

Geraldine smothered a yawn.

'I've never seen her there before!' said Tara.

'Yawn, yawn,' said Geraldine.

'Thing *is* . . .'

'What?' said Geraldine. 'What is the thing?'

'Well, I know we don't particularly *like* her. I mean, she's okay . . .'

Geraldine sniffed.

Lily, cautiously, said, 'I don't think she likes *us*.'

'Why shouldn't she like us?' Geraldine turned on Lily, indignantly. 'What's wrong with us?'

'We haven't got famous dads,' said Tara.

'Her dad isn't famous!'

'He is quite.'

'Just because he's written some stupid pop song—'

'*Love me do.*' Tara, unable to resist the temptation, was immediately on her feet and bopping about. '*Love me do, like I love you! Baby, it hurts when you turn away—*'

'Oh, please!' begged Geraldine, clapping her hands to her ears.

It was true that Tara's voice, though loud, was not the most tuneful. But it was a good song, thought Lily. It wasn't fair to say it was stupid just because it had been written by Daniela's dad.

Geraldine said, 'Elvis Presley is famous. Tommy Steele is famous. Who's ever heard of Tony Sabatini?'

Tara sniggered. 'You, obviously!'

'Only because we're stuck with his stupid self-important daughter!'

'She's not that bad,' said Tara. 'She was quite friendly down the club.'

'I hope you didn't butter her up?'

'Of course I didn't butter her up! I just said hello in a perfectly normal fashion, same as anyone would, and she said hello back, and I said I'd never seen her there before, so she said that was because it was the first time she'd come, and then she introduced me to this boy Cameron and said it had been his idea, cos he'd heard it was quite good, and I said it *was* quite good, and she said maybe they might come again, and how long had I been going there, and I said—'

Geraldine's eyes were already starting to roll. Lily gave a little giggle.

'I said about six months, so she said did I go to St

Luke's, cos it's, like, you know, attached to the church, so I said I used to go to Sunday school when I was little and she wanted to know whether they minded if you didn't go there and I said no, everyone was welcome, and if she came next week we were going to have a quiz evening and—' Tara broke off and stared accusingly at Lily. 'What's so funny?'

'Sorry!' Lily hiccupped. 'Go on!'

In tones of cold dignity Tara said, 'That's it. That's all we said.'

'Well, you had a really sparkling conversation,' said Geraldine.

'I was just trying to be friendly! I thought if I could, like . . . establish relations, she might decide we weren't so bad and invite us to her next birthday party. And don't tell me,' said Tara, 'that you wouldn't go if you had the chance!'

'Oh, I'd probably *go*,' said Geraldine. 'Just to be nosy.'

'I'd go,' said Lily.

'Anyone would that's got any sense! Know who went to her last one? This skiffle group, friends of her dad. And boys! Loads of them!'

Lily thought about it. A *few* boys would be good, but loads of them? That might be a bit scary! She wasn't sure what you were supposed to talk to them about. All Thomas wanted to talk about was Dan Dare and space travel. Of course, Thomas was only twelve years old; the boys that went to Daniela's birthday party would be at least thirteen. Maybe even fourteen. Even fifteen. She would be tongue-tied! But then again, thought Lily, everyone had to start somewhere. Tara and Geraldine obviously didn't have any problems finding things to talk about. Maybe she would be able to pick up a few tips – except that Daniela was never in a million years going to invite any of them to one of her parties. She was far too grand!

'Know what?' said Tara. 'If you invited her to *your* party . . .'

'Mine?' said Lily.

'Yes! You invite her, then she'll have to invite you back!'

'She wouldn't have to invite you or me,' said Geraldine.

'She wouldn't *have* to, but she might. I mean, if she starts coming to the club and I keep on being friendly . . .'

'You mean, you keep on buttering her up!'

'It'd be worth it,' said Tara, earnestly. 'Just to meet boys!' She turned back to Lily. 'If you could just send her an invitation . . .'

'I can't,' said Lily.

'What d'you mean, you can't?'

'I can't! I'm not having a party this time.'

Tara stared at her, eyes wide in disbelief. They always had parties!

'I thought it would be more of a treat if we went out for a meal,' said Lily. 'Just the three of us! Plus, Mum and Dad, of course. And Thomas, I *suppose*. Honestly,' she said, 'it'll be fun!' People were always having parties, but how many times did anyone go out for a meal? She didn't know anyone who ever had! 'Mum said we could go to that new Wimpy Bar that just opened.'

'Hmm.' Tara considered the idea. 'Would be something different,' she agreed.

'That's exactly what I thought,' said Lily. 'It was Mum's idea!'

'More to the point,' said Geraldine, 'what made you decide you didn't want a party?'

'Just don't. Felt like doing something different.'

Geraldine nodded, wisely. 'You mean, after last year.'

Lily's party last year had been a disaster. Auntie Marjorie had turned up without even being asked. She had brought the Little Angel with her. The Little Angel had immediately taken over, like it was *her* party, twirling about in her horrible icky party dress, all pink and sparkly, with a bow in her hair, showing off in front of everyone.

Mum had said, 'I'm so sorry, Lily! It won't happen again, I promise you.'

All very well Mum *saying* that, but what were they

supposed to do if Auntie Marjorie just turned up on the doorstep again? Especially if she came with an extra-special present, like last year, when she had brought a huge bundle of Derwent pencil crayons, in all different colours.

'A little bird told me you were collecting them, so I checked with your mum which ones you still needed . . . I think now you'll find you have the whole set!'

It was true that for months Lily had been painstakingly buying herself just one pencil per week, which was as much as her pocket money would run to – well, if she wanted any left over for sweets or books or hair slides. Beautiful as they were, though, all massed together, it hadn't been worth the shame and embarrassment of having to put up with the Little Angel bopping and bouncing all over the place.

'Going out for a meal will be something different,' she pleaded.

'Oh, 'it'll be *different;* it just won't help with boys!'

Reproachfully Geraldine said, 'Not everything revolves around boys. We shall be perfectly happy without them.'

'Just the three of us,' said Lily. 'I'm looking forward to it!'

And then, horror of horrors, Auntie Marjorie actually rang up and suggested that she and the Little Angel might come as well! Lily heard her on the phone talking to Mum. She heard Mum say, 'Just going for a meal this year. Something a bit more grown-up.' And then she heard Auntie Marjorie, whose voice, Dad always said, could shatter a glass a mile away, 'Lovely! We'll come and join you.'

'*Mu-u-um!*' Lily gave a strangulated yelp. Mum put a finger to her lips and shook her head.

'I'm not sure they'd be able to squeeze you in at this late date . . . places tend to get crowded on a Saturday. I'll give them a quick ring and see, but I honestly don't hold out much hope.'

Lily, in silent agony, mouthed, '*Mum!*'

'It's all right.' Mum put the phone back down. 'You

can relax! I'll make sure they can't squeeze anyone else in. No harm in the occasional white lie!'

'But suppose they just turn up?'

'They won't just turn up! They won't know where we're going. You do realise, of course –' Mum said it slyly – 'you won't get a bumper birthday present like you had last year?'

For just a moment Lily wondered if she ought to feel guilty. Auntie Marjorie had gone to such trouble, getting Mum to check which colours she already had and which she still needed. It had been one of the best presents anyone had ever given her! Geraldine had been quite jealous when she had heard.

They were so beautiful that Lily had hardly dared to use them. She couldn't bear the thought of wearing her favourite colours down to stumps! They were all still there, brand new and shiny, arranged in their proper order in their box on her bedroom mantelpiece.

'I could always ring back to say they *can* find room,' teased Mum.

'But then she wouldn't just bring my birthday present,' said Lily, 'she'd bring Smelly Mellie as well!'

Mum agreed that that was the drawback.

'I don't think I could bear it!' said Lily. In any case, Auntie Marjorie normally sent her a book token, and she needed a book token to buy the latest Enid Blyton. She had a whole collection of Enid Blytons as well. Geraldine claimed, rather grandly, to have 'grown out of that sort of thing', but she was always quite happy to borrow them from Lily – even if only to say, in her superior fashion, that it was 'really just kids' stuff'.

'So . . . what do I do?' said Mum. 'Do I tell a little white lie or—'

'Little white lie!' said Lily.

She already had that bossy Dandelion Head threatening to mess around with her life. The last thing she needed was the Little Angel turning up and ruining everything!

CHAPTER
7

Lily was almost beginning to think that a birthday meal with Geraldine and Tara might really be better than a party – even a party *not* gatecrashed by Auntie Marjorie and the Little Angel. Parties were fun, of course, but more fun, she sometimes thought, if they were other people's rather than your own. When it was your own you were expected to greet everyone and say thank you very much as you stood there unwrapping presents, with everyone watching and waiting for you to make appreciative comments. 'Ooh, lovely!' or 'Just what I wanted!' Lily sometimes found it a bit embarrassing. Of course she still had to thank Geraldine and Tara for their presents – an autograph book from Geraldine and a piggy bank from Tara – but that was all right. That was only Geraldine and Tara! They didn't count. She had known them so long they were almost like family. Tara, in any case, was so excited at being in a restaurant she hardly gave Lily a chance to assure her that the piggy bank was 'Exactly what I wanted!' She had obviously become reconciled to the thought of no boys. Much to Dad's obvious amazement she chattered and giggled practically non-stop from the moment she sat down. Geraldine as usual rolled her eyes, but Dad just shook his head as if bemused. He seemed, if anything, to find it funny.

Geraldine, no doubt feeling that some kind of apology was called for, took it upon herself to explain. 'She has this nervous affliction, I'm afraid.'

Dad said, 'Oh, so that's what it is!'

Tara, indignantly, said, 'Who has a nervous affection?'

'You have,' said Geraldine. 'Keeping on staring at that waiter!'

Tara giggled. 'He's cute!'

Lily supposed that he was, quite – though nowhere near as cute as the boy with blue eyes! She found herself lapsing into a happy daydream where it was the boy with the blue eyes who was the waiter, and he came up to their table and said he had heard it was her birthday, and started singing 'Happy Birthday' – *'Happy birthday to you, happy birthday to you, happy birthday, dear Lillee!'* – and everyone in the restaurant turned to look at her, and at the end the boy snatched a rose from one of the vases on the table and presented it to her, and kissed her hand and everyone broke into applause, and—

'It really isn't her fault,' said Geraldine. 'She's not used to being let out.'

Lily came to with a start. Who wasn't used to being let out? What was she talking about? Was she talking about Lily? Crimson-faced, Lily dived under the table and began fiddling with the strap on her shoe. Had she given herself away? Had she said something, without realising?

'Just behave yourself,' said Geraldine, giving Tara a bit of a shove.

Tara pulled a face. 'Yes, miss. Sorry, miss!' And then, with an impish grin, to Dad, 'She doesn't like having to be seen in public with me.'

'No,' said Geraldine, 'because you're a disgrace!'

Tara smirked.

Mum, in kindly tones, said, 'Don't let it worry you, Geraldine! And you, Thomas, stop eating with your mouth open! And take your elbows off the table. For goodness' sake! Show some manners.'

'Blimey,' said Thomas. 'They're having a go at me now as well!'

Afterwards, when they had taken Geraldine and Tara home, and Thomas, complaining bitterly, had been packed off to bed, Dad said, 'Geraldine's a very high-minded young lady, isn't she? Have to be on your best behaviour with that one!'

'She's always so serious, isn't she?' said Mum.

'She can't help it!' Lily was quick to leap to Geraldine's

defence. 'She's just so much cleverer than the rest of us.'

'Wouldn't surprise me if we were looking at a future prime minister,' said Dad.

'Woman prime minister?' Lily wondered what Miss Carpenter would have to say. She would probably say that all things were possible. *Aim high, girls! Aim high!*

'Bound to happen sooner or later,' said Dad. 'Way things are going. Women on the buses, women on the trains . . . Give it a few years and your mate Geraldine'll be up there, in Westminster, telling us all what to do!'

'I'd like to think so,' said Mum.

Lily, growing interested, said, 'What about Tara?'

Dad chuckled. 'Nothing high-minded about that one!'

'A bit of a live wire,' agreed Mum.

'Oh, there's no harm in her. She'll settle down.'

'Settle down how?' said Lily. 'You mean, like getting married and having babies and being a housewife?'

'And why not?' said Dad. 'What's wrong with being a housewife?'

Lily pulled a face. *Remember, girls, this is the twentieth century!*

'They couldn't be more different, could they?' said Dad. 'The two of them . . . Little Miss Prune and Little Miss Giggle!'

Lily would have liked to ask Dad 'What about me?' but felt suddenly shy. It was left to Mum to ask it for her: 'What about Lily?'

'Oh, well, Lily!' Dad gave her a hug. 'She'll be everyone's sweetheart! Cute little face like that . . . who could resist?'

'Actually, as a matter of fact,' said Lily, 'I'm going to have a career.'

What sort of career she hadn't yet decided, but there had to be something she was good at.

'Every single girl in this class,' Miss Carpenter had once informed them, 'has her own unique abilities. It's simply a question of identifying them.'

'I'm not just going to leave school and get married,' said Lily. 'I'm going to *do* something!'

'Heard that one before,' said Dad. 'Your mum's a prime example!'

'That's true.' Mum gave a little sigh. 'I was all set to go to college when I met your dad.'

'And immediately got swept off your feet!'

'I did,' said Mum. 'Though blown off course might be another way of putting it.'

'So what would you have done,' said Lily, 'if you hadn't married Dad?'

'Turned into a sour old maid!' said Dad.

'*Dad!*'

Dad threw up his hands. 'Just kidding, just kidding!'

'Would you have had a career?' said Lily.

'I don't know about a career . . . I'd probably still have ended up as a housewife with a couple of kids. One did in those days; it was what was expected. With some jobs you were actually forced to give them up if they found out you were married! Fortunately, it's a bit different now, so if Lily wants to have a career, then I say good for her!'

'I'd probably want to get married as well,' said Lily, rather anxiously. Even Miss Carpenter didn't have anything against people getting married. *Or* having babies. Just so long as they didn't assume that was all they could do.

The only problem was that if you wanted to get married, you had to find someone to get married to, and how was she supposed to do that when she never met any boys and wouldn't know what to say to them if she did? Imagine if by some miracle Daniela decided to ask them to her party and there were all those boys, dozens of them, and Lily spent the entire time hiding away in a corner, too shy to come out, while people like Tara chattered and giggled and no one even noticed that Lily was there!

She sometimes seriously worried that she wasn't quite normal. Not only did she have no idea how to speak to boys, she didn't even seem to have crushes on them the same as other people. Before she had started hanging out with Derek, Tara had had a new crush practically every week. Even now (in spite of Derek) she would open her weekly *Picturegoer* magazine and swoon dramatically over the photo of some film star.

Even Geraldine had once admitted that she had 'a bit of a thing' about someone. Everybody had widened their eyes and gone, 'Oooh! Who?' He was called Mario, said Geraldine, and he was a singer. Daniela (sounding a bit jealous, in case he might turn out to be more famous than her dad) had wanted to know whether he was someone they would have heard of. Geraldine, in her schoolteacherly way, had said, 'I would certainly hope so!'

'So what does he sing? What's your favourite song that he sings?'

Geraldine, eagerly, had said, 'Well, one of the roles he's most famous for is Radames, in *Aida*,' at which there had been a rather long pause and Daniela had said, '*Opera?*' and they had all dutifully groaned and rolled their eyes. Trust Geraldine!

But at least, thought Lily, she had confessed to having

a bit of a thing, even if it *was* about an opera singer. Lily had never had a bit of a thing about anyone! She had once tried very hard to convince herself that she had romantic feelings for a boy called Trevor, who lived in her road, but it hadn't really worked. Not even though he was two years older than Lily, and – according to her mum – 'Such a handsome young man!' Instead of making her feel all warm and gooey, the thought of being kissed by him just made her feel sick. The only boy she could imagine kissing was the boy with the blue eyes, and he wasn't real. Not properly real. Not if Dandelion Head were to be believed. If Dandelion Head was telling the truth, and not simply acting a part, then he belonged in the future, the same as she did. Dad, of course, would just laugh. Time travel, space rockets, men on the moon . . . *That'll be the day!* But Thomas had said that it would definitely happen, and Thomas had done some serious reading. She sometimes thought, when it came to scientific possibilities, that Thomas actually knew more than Dad.

Meanwhile, she was still waiting for Dandelion Head to reappear. Where had she got to? She would be back, she had said – but could she be relied upon? It would be typical, thought Lily, if she went and got the date wrong again and ended up years too late, or years too early. Imagine if she arrived in 1854, before Lily was even born! Or *2054*, when Lily would be . . . She worked it out on her fingers. Over a hundred! For all she knew the wretched girl might actually have tried. She really didn't seem to have a clue what she was doing.

It was all nonsense, anyway! How could anyone come back from the future? The more Lily thought about it, the more ridiculous it seemed. They might be *working* on it – they might even be conducting secret experiments. But that didn't mean it was actually happening!

Or did it?

Could it?

No, thought Lily, rather crossly. It couldn't! How could it be happening without anyone knowing? The government would know! The government knew every-thing. It was their job to know. And if the government knew, then the newspapers would find out and there would be headlines in Dad's paper: **TIME TRAVEL! ARE YOU BEING SPIED ON?** And Thomas would be all jubilant – *Told you so!* – and Dad would have to eat his words. But there hadn't been any headlines, and Lily was really starting to resent the way Dandelion Head was using her. Making up all this rubbish! *She* might call it improvisation; some people would say it was nothing more than telling great whopping lies. Did she go into school every day and have a giggle about it? 'I'm pretending to come from the future and this simpleton actually believes me!'

She had assured Lily – *watch my lips!* – that she didn't go to Spotlight, but that was obviously just another great whopping lie. You couldn't place any reliance on what she said. Any of it! Except . . .

Doubts still remained. That conjuring trick with the photograph – the way she just suddenly appeared and then equally suddenly disappeared. How did she *do* it?

Lily had almost started to give up hope of ever finding out. She still had her daydreams, but she knew, in her heart, that that was all they were: just daydreams. They couldn't ever come true. Her heart no longer raced in expectation, as she went into town with Mum and Dad on a Saturday morning, that at any moment she might bump into the boy with the blue eyes – that he might recognise her, and smile, and say hello; that Dad would chuckle and ask 'So who was that handsome young man?' and Thomas would go, 'Lily's got a boyfriend, Lily's got a boyfriend!' And Mum would tell Auntie Marjorie on the telephone that 'It was so sweet, the way he smiled at her!'

It had seemed possible once. She knew, after all, that *he* wasn't just a figment. Tara and Geraldine had both seen him. He had even spoken! But then so had Dandelion Head. Dandelion Head almost never *stopped* speaking! So she wasn't just a figment either. But even now Lily still didn't know for sure where she actually came from. If she really belonged to the future, impossible though that might seem, did that mean they both did?

One thing was certain, if Dandelion Head didn't come back to answer Lily's questions, she would never know.

CHAPTER 8

Lily was wandering home, one afternoon at the end of school, when all of a sudden Dandelion Head reappeared. It took Lily by surprise. She had almost given up expecting ever to see Dandelion again.

She said, 'Oh! It's you!'

Dandelion came sauntering towards her, a big smile on her face.

'See? I told you I'd be back! I reckon I'm really starting to get the hang of things!'

'Pity you couldn't have got back a bit earlier,' grumbled Lily.

'Why?' said Dandelion. 'Did you miss me?'

'Not specially,' said Lily. 'Why should I miss you?'

'I'd miss *you* if you didn't turn up!'

Lily said, 'Huh!'

'Don't be such a grump! Let's go and sit on our seat.'

'It's not our seat,' said Lily. 'It's for people waiting for buses.'

'Yes, and there aren't any! Either we go and sit down or I'll disappear again.' She grinned. 'I bet you've been wondering how I do that!'

'Not really,' said Lily. (She was beginning to tell as many great whopping lies as Dandelion Head!) 'It just seemed like bad manners.'

'Yeah. Well! We're not supposed to just disappear. *Or* spring up out of nowhere. We're supposed to blend in. Not supposed to frighten people. Not that I'm *supposed* to be here at all . . . Hey, but did you notice? I didn't just jump out at you, did I? Got that one cracked! It's a question of having a bit more control. Not as easy as you might think. It can sometimes make you feel a bit funny moving from one time to another. Travel sickness! Most people get used to it sooner or later. Anyway!' She patted the seat next to her. 'That's better! I suppose you're waiting to hear about *him*?'

'I want to know who he is!'

'I'll tell you who he *was*. Want to know who he was?'

'I . . .' Lily faltered. 'You don't mean . . .'

'Who he *was*,' said Dandelion Head, venomously, 'was my boyfriend.'

Lily said, 'W-was?'

'Was,' said Dandelion.

'Oh! You mean, he isn't any more?'

'I wouldn't have him now,' said Dandelion Head, 'if he went down on his bended knees and begged me! Want to know why?'

Lily nodded, trying not to appear too eager.

'I'll tell you why! Because this girl that used to be my best friend but is now my deadliest enemy in the whole world got her hooks into him and won't let go, and he's like all pathetic and can't stand up to her, and she's just making eyes at him and digging her claws in deeper and deeper . . . *Oh, Luki!*' Dandelion Head put on a silly little voice. '*Oh, Luki, I love you, I love you . . .*'

'Luki?' said Lily, entranced. 'Is that his name?'

Dandelion Head looked annoyed, as if she hadn't meant to say it.

'What's *her* name?'

'Serissa.' Dandelion Head curled her lip. 'Stupid name for a stupid person!'

Lily privately thought it rather pretty, but decided it was probably best not to say so.

'That,' said Dandelion Head, 'is why he slipped through after me while my back was turned. Wouldn't have been bold enough to do it by himself! She'll have put him up to it . . . *Oh, Luki, do go back and check!*'

'Check what?'

'That the timeline's still holding. That you're still due to be his great-grandmother!'

Rather crossly, Lily said, 'That's ridiculous!'

'Not according to the timeline . . . Well, *one* timeline.'

'You mean there's more?'

'Oh, an infinity! It all depends on your meeting a Certain Person, getting married to that Certain Person—'

'I'm going to get *married*?' said Lily.

'I said it all depends. Pay attention! I can't keep repeating myself. You get married to him. You have children. Yes?'

Lily nodded, uncertainly.

'Right! So then your children have children, and your children's children have children, and, hey presto! Before you know it, you're a great-grandmother. *His* great-grandmother. On the other hand –' Dandelion paused, to let it sink in – 'if none of that happens, it means he simply won't exist. Well, not in this timeline. Not if I have my way. Which I can assure you,' said Dandelion, 'I intend to. And then won't she be sorry!'

'Are you saying,' said Lily, 'that you would actually just—'

'Delete him! Happens all the time. It's a game we used to play . . . *In and out the timelines, see the people go—*'

'You mean, he just wouldn't be here any more?'

'Oh, don't worry – he'd still be *somewhere*. Just not here!'

'But I thought you were in love with him?'

Dandelion scowled. 'I never said I was in love with him. Said he was my boyfriend. But if I can't have him, she's certainly not going to! Horrid scheming thing. Honestly, boys are so feeble, the way they let themselves be manipulated! It's pathetic. Especially with someone like that! Just boring, boring, boring! Looks like a doll. See for yourself!'

Dandelion Head did the tapping thing on her wrist and a picture immediately flashed up, hovering in mid-air.

'How do you do that?' said Lily.

'Never mind how I do it! Just—'

'Is it some kind of conjuring trick?'

'Yeah, let's call it a conjuring trick. You wouldn't be able to grasp it, even if I told you. Just look at the picture!'

Obediently, Lily looked. She saw a small, rather pretty girl with short hair cut in a fringe.

'See what I mean?' Dandelion Head tapped again on her wrist and the picture disappeared. 'Just a totally *boring* little person. Goodness only knows what he sees in her. Like I said, she'll have been the one that pushed him to come . . . *Just go and do a quick check! See what the future holds!*'

'What future?' Nothing this girl said made any sense! 'I thought *you* were the future?'

'I may be *your* future – I'm not *our* future. *Our* future's yet to come.'

'So why not go *there* and check? Why come back here?'

'Future's not so easy to get into. They've had too many people trying to steal ideas and smuggle them back, pretend they've invented stuff. Make a name for themselves.'

'Well, but I don't see,' said Lily, 'how you can check

what the future's going to hold by going back to the past. Doesn't make any sense at all!'

'Actually, it does,' said Dandelion Head. 'At least –' she gave another of her cackles – 'it does if no one starts pulling on threads and unravelling everything! *He* thinks if he comes back and checks whether certain things have happened that are supposed to have happened, then he'll know for sure who his great-grandmother's going to be and whether he still gets to exist in this timeline and whether he and she stay together. Except –' she gave another of her exultant cackles – 'he came back too early! That'll teach him – and her! Honestly, can you imagine –' Dandelion Head said it in tones of deepest scorn – 'can you imagine *anyone* preferring her to me? I mean, what's she got going for her? Absolutely nothing! Have you ever seen anything so boring?'

'Maybe,' said Lily, 'she has a nice personality?'

'*Personality?* She hasn't got any personality!'

'Oh. Well. In that case—'

'She needn't think I'm letting *her* end up with him!'

'You're very vengeful,' said Lily.

'Of course I'm vengeful! Wouldn't you be if your so-called *best friend* went and stole your boyfriend?'

Lily tried to imagine it. First off, she had to imagine *having* a boyfriend. She felt her cheeks colour up. 'Did you say his name was Luki?'

'Yeah! So what?'

'And he thinks I'm going to be his great-grandmother, but I'm actually not?'

'Not if I have anything to do with it!' Dandelion Head looked at Lily, searchingly. 'You surely don't *want* to be his great-grandmother? *Do* you?'

Lily, feeling rather uncomfortable, muttered that she supposed not.

'*I* wouldn't! Hardly very romantic. Just imagine! You'd be old and grey and wrinkled, while he'd still be young and beautiful! Is that what you want?'

'Well, n-no. But I'd like to be *someone's* great-grandmother!'

'Really?'

'Well, yes! Cos I mean . . . before I was a *great*-*grand*mother I'd be a *grand*mother, and if I was a *grand*mother, it'd mean I'd got married and had a family!'

'You want to get married.' Dandelion Head nodded. 'Of course! It's what people do, isn't it? In the twentieth century. It's all right – you'll still get married. I'll find someone for you!'

Lily bristled. 'Think I can't find someone for myself?'

'There's no need to snap my head off,' said Dandelion. 'I'm only trying to be helpful.'

'I'm sure that's very good of you,' said Lily, doing her best to sound like Geraldine.

'Well, you know –' Dandelion shrugged – 'I feel sort of responsible for you. I won't abandon you! I promise! You have my word. I'll be back in good time!'

'Good time for what?' said Lily. She narrowed her eyes. 'Is something going to happen?'

'I should hope so!' Dandelion gave a happy chortle. 'Sad to be fourteen without something happening! Just have to wait and see what the timeline holds. Don't worry, we'll talk more when I come back. Maybe we'll be able to have a proper conversation at last!'

'I'm not sure I want a conversation,' said Lily. 'What do we need a conversation for?'

'Well . . . get to know each other a bit better.'

'I don't want to get to know you! I don't see why you have to come here at all! Keeping on bothering me.'

'*Bothering* you?' Dandelion sounded quite hurt. 'I thought we were getting on rather well!'

'But why are you *here*?'

'Have to be on the spot,' said Dandelion. 'Can't just click on a remote! It doesn't work like that.'

Lily was about to say 'What doesn't work?' but instead, primly, she said, 'You can't have *a* remote. "Remote" is an adjective, not a noun!' Geraldine would be proud of her! So would Miss Carpenter. 'You have to say, a remote *something*.'

'All right, so you can't just pick up a remote something and press a button! If it was that easy, it'd be total chaos. Everyone would be at it! You have to make *some* effort.'

'To do what? Exactly?'

'Make things happen! Or not happen, as the case may be.'

'What sort of things?'

A shifty look stole over Dandelion's face. 'Just things.'

'To do with me?' Dandelion waved an airy hand. Crossly Lily said, 'You'd just better not try interfering with my life!'

'Why?' said Dandelion. 'What do you think you can do about it?' And then, relenting, 'Don't worry, it's nothing bad! Just one tiny little tweak. So tiny it will hardly even cause a ripple. Far as you're concerned, you won't notice anything different. Life will go on just the same. Happens all the time! Little tweaks here and there.'

'You mean, people coming back and messing with other people's lives!'

Dandelion shrugged.

'Don't you have rules and regulations?'

'Of course there are *rules*. But they can't keep track of every little thread that breaks! Obviously if you went and wiped out someone really famous, like, say, the guy that discovered penicillin—'

'Alexander Fleming,' said Lily, pleased with herself for remembering.

'Yeah. Or Florence Nightingale or – or Napoleon, or someone, they'd be on to it in a flash! But just changing the odd little thing here and there . . . there's no way they can keep track! Nothing ever stands still. Even without people interfering. *The threads of time, they bend and break* . . . a little jingle we learn when we're young. Think of it this way: it's like you're living in the middle of an enormous web and—'

'Not a spider's web?' Lily wasn't too keen on spiders, especially not the great big hairy sort that sometimes galloped across her bedroom ceiling, forcing her to cower under the blankets in case they fell on her. She didn't like the thought of living in the middle of a spider's web!

'*Any* web,' said Dandelion. 'Just a web! Threads get

broken all the time. Mostly it just creates minor ripples, hardly worth bothering with. Nobody would ever check. It's just that now and again something major happens and it throws the whole timeline out. That's when you can get blown off course!'

Mum had said that meeting Dad had blown her off course. Did that mean some interfering busybody like Dandelion Head had messed with Mum's life?

'Anyway,' said Dandelion, 'I've told you what you wanted to know, I'm going to go now.' She stood up. 'I'm going to do it really s-l-o-w-l-y . . . just for you. See? Watch!'

Obediently, Lily watched as Dandelion Head wandered off in the direction of Barclay Road. She watched as she rounded the corner. Scarcely seconds later, when Lily herself jumped up and raced across to check, she had disappeared. Barclay Road was completely empty; not a trace of her.

Just to make sure, Lily walked down as far as Spotlight. A couple of girls were coming out. Made suddenly bold,

Lily said, 'Excuse me? You don't happen to know someone with bright yellow hair cut in spikes? Looks like a dandelion?'

The minute she said it, she wanted the earth to swallow her up, but the girls didn't seem to find it a particularly strange question. At any rate, they didn't snigger or stare as if Lily were a bit loopy. One of them, in doubtful tones, said, 'There's Jody Hansen . . . she's just dyed her hair green. Used to be pink. Not in spikes, though.'

'Why?' said the other girl. 'Did you think she was at Spotlight?'

'I thought perhaps she might be,' said Lily.

'No.' They shook their heads quite firmly. 'No one like that. Sorry!'

The two of them went on their way. Lily was left amazed – and just a little impressed – by her own boldness. She had done what Tara had wanted her to do right back at the beginning: she had actually spoken to some students from Spotlight! Not that it had achieved very much. Nothing at all, really. Dandelion Head had told her over and over that she didn't go there. It seemed, after all, that she had been telling the truth. But if she was telling the truth about that . . . Lily simply didn't know what to believe!

CHAPTER
9

'Do you honestly think,' said Lily, arriving home to find Thomas in the kitchen, helping himself from a packet of custard creams, 'what we were talking about the other day—'

'Yes?' Thomas crammed a biscuit into his mouth and turned to her, eagerly. 'About time travel?' Crumbs sprayed out.

Lily took a step backwards. Really, he had the manners of a pig! But he did know about time travel – or at least, the professor obviously did.

'Do you *honestly* think people could come back and mess with our lives?'

'I reckon they could change things.'

'Even in spite of rules saying they weren't allowed to?'

'Yeah, well, rules! Just there to be broken, aren't they? Like people that go burgling. Might be a law against it – doesn't stop 'em doing it.'

'Hmm.' Lily thought about it. 'So if someone came back from the future and wanted to change stuff, how do you think they'd do it? I mean, like, when you said suppose Mum and Dad had never met – if they hadn't gone to that party—'

'You and me wouldn't be here!'

'I get that,' said Lily. 'But how would they make it happen? How could they stop Mum and Dad going to a party?'

'Easy! All sorts of ways. Could just have someone tell Dad it had been cancelled. Or Mum could trip over and twist her ankle, or—'

'But how would they do it?'

'Oh, they'd find a way! If they really wanted. Give Mum a bit of a shove while she was walking up the High Street on Saturday morning . . . Loads of people about.

No one'd notice. Quite easy when you stop to think about it.'

It would certainly be easy enough for Dandelion Head – and just the sort of trick she might play. Lily made a mental note to be on her guard at all times.

'Course, they'd be in trouble if anyone found out,' said Thomas. 'They wouldn't do it just for fun.'

'So what do you think would make them?'

'I guess they'd have their reasons. Like if they really, really didn't want someone to be born – Napoleon, for instance – they could always come back and make sure their parents didn't meet. Not that they would with Napoleon, cos that would be too obvious. Could only do it with ordinary people.'

'You mean, like Mum and Dad.'

'Any of us!'

'So do you think they'd actually have to *be* here? They couldn't stay in the future and do it from there?'

'Like a remote-control kind of thing?' Thomas shook his head. 'Wouldn't have thought so.'

'But you reckon they could come here and do it?'

''Cording to the professor, they already are.'

'Is that what he said? That they're coming back and messing with people's lives?'

'Said they *could* if they felt like it. Most of 'em probably wouldn't. More likely just want to have a look around. The professor reckons they'll have been at it for years without anyone knowing.'

'It's a bit frightening, really,' said Lily. 'When you think about it.'

'Frightening? What's frightening about it?'

'Not knowing if someone might suddenly do something that'd change the course of your life!'

Thomas, obviously not bothered, helped himself to another biscuit. That, thought Lily, was almost a whole packet he'd eaten.

'Don't really see,' said Thomas through a mouthful of biscuit, 'that it's any different from how it's always been. It's just that now you happen to be aware of it.'

'Yes, and I'd rather not be,' said Lily. And then, struck

by a new thought, she added: 'Do you suppose, sometimes, some of them might decide to stay?'

'Shouldn't think so,' said Thomas. 'What'd they want to do that for?'

'Well, I don't know!' She gave an embarrassed giggle. 'Like maybe if they met someone and . . .'

'What?'

'Fell in love with them maybe?' She felt her cheeks fire up as she said it. *You're his great-grandmother!* But she wasn't; she wasn't! That only happened in the future. Unless . . . unless the timeline were to change! If the timeline changed, things might all work out quite differently. They might just be a normal boy and girl meeting each other in the twentieth century. It could happen! According to Dandelion, timelines were changing all the time.

Thomas huffed, impatiently.

'There's no reason it couldn't happen!' said Lily. 'And if it did, then they wouldn't want to go back! Not unless they could take the person with them. Would that be possible, d'you think?'

'No idea,' said Thomas.

'What does the professor say?'

'Doesn't say anything,' said Thomas. 'He's a *professor*. He's not interested in all that slurpy stuff! Scientific possibilities,' said Thomas, 'that's what he deals with. Space travel, time travel—'

'Men on the moon!' Mum had come into the room. 'Are they up there yet?' She laughed. Lily saw that she had Mr Peachey with her. Mr Peachey was their neighbour. He was very old. He had been their neighbour for as long as Lily could remember. He always said that Lily and Thomas were like the grandchildren he had never had.

'Thomas is convinced,' said Mum, 'that give it a year or two we'll be blasting men into space!'

Thomas protested. 'I never said a year or two! Decades, more like.'

'Aha! And then what?' said Mr Peachey. 'First stop, the moon. Next stop, Mars?'

'Could be,' said Thomas.

'So, tell us the truth . . . is Mars really full of little green men?'

'We don't yet know,' said Thomas, rather sternly, 'whether it's full of *any* kind of men. Might just be microbes.'

'But they will be green!'

'Why?' said Thomas. He was beginning to sound slightly irritated. 'Why's it always green? Why not blue or brown or—'

'Yes, yes!' Mum intervened, hastily. 'Let's not go into all that now. Mr Peachey's in a bit of a rush.'

'That's right.' Mr Peachey pulled a face. 'Dentist's appointment. I just stopped by to check that you were both coming to my party?'

'Of course they are!' said Mum. 'An eightieth birthday is not an occasion to be missed! They'll be there.'

'Jolly good!' Mr Peachey put a bony arm round each of them. Lily tried not to wriggle. 'That's the ticket!'

'We're looking forward to it,' said Lily. 'We want to see you blow out your candles!'

'Aha! So that means there's going to be a cake, eh?'

'Mum's already made one,' said Lily. 'I helped her!'

'Call that helping?' Mum gave her a little push. 'Hanging about the kitchen waiting to lick the mixing bowl?'

'That,' said Thomas, 'is disgusting!'

Mum said, 'Yes, like stealing bits of icing off the top while you thought my back was turned!'

'It was round the side,' said Thomas. 'Just the drips, that's all. I was *tidying* it for you. And it was me,' he added, 'that did the candles. Wasn't room for eighty, so I said why not arrange them in two little circles –' he drew a picture in the air – 'one on top of the other, make 'em *look* like eighty.'

'Still a lot to blow out,' said Lily.

Mr Peachey nodded in agreement. 'Just have to hope I can manage it. At my age, you know, one runs out of puff! Still, at least it will be something to raise a smile. Otherwise, I fear, it won't really be a young person's idea of fun . . . just a bunch of old fogeys sitting around nattering.'

After Mr Peachey had gone, Thomas said, 'Is the party really just going to be a bunch of old fogeys?'

'Absolutely not!' said Mum.

'So who's coming?'

Mum smiled, triumphantly. 'Far more people than Mr Peachey imagines! I managed to get a list from his old school, and a surprising number of his former pupils have said they're going to turn up and bring their wives and children. He was obviously very well respected. He was headmaster for almost twenty years, you know.'

'Can't see me wanting to go to old Bagshot's eightieth birthday,' said Thomas.

'Can't see Mr Bagshot wanting you to!' retorted Mum. 'I pity anyone that's your headmaster!'

Thomas said, 'Huh!' And then, obviously still feeling disgruntled about the little green men on Mars, 'Don't suppose it'll be much fun, people being all old and everything.'

'Not everybody'll be old,' said Lily.

'And you're still going,' said Mum, as she left the room.

'Didn't say I wasn't! Just said it prob'ly won't be much of a laugh.'

'Don't worry,' said Lily. 'You can always take a packet of biscuits with you. Stand in a corner and eat the lot! Whole *packet*,' she said.

Thomas scowled. 'Wasn't the whole packet. It was already open.'

'Yeah, and who opened it?'

'What's it to you?'

'I just had to stand here and get blasted by biscuit crumbs!'

'Boohoo! And incidentally,' said Thomas, 'for your information and as a matter of interest, I don't think people *could* come back here and stay. Not even –' his lip curled – 'if they did *fall in lurve*.'

Lily bristled. 'Why not? Why couldn't they?'

'Well, think about it,' said Thomas. 'How would they manage? They wouldn't know how anything works. It'd be like if we went back to the Stone Age – we'd never survive!'

'The Stone Age was *primitive*.'

'So what do you think we are?'

Lily munched doubtfully on her bottom lip. She remembered what Dandelion had said: *you're still very primitive*.

'They wouldn't understand how anything works!' Thomas went on. 'They'd be used to just pressing buttons, or saying *do this, do that*. They'd go and sit in cars and tell them to go somewhere and wonder why they didn't move, or stand in the kitchen going, *Food! Get me some food!* and expecting it to just suddenly appear out of nowhere, or—'

'Yes, all *right*,' said Lily, crossly. 'I get it!'

'It just makes you realise how far behind we are. Like children, really. That's probably how they think of us. I mean, it stands to reason, they've got to be far more advanced than we are, I mean—'

'I said *all right*,' said Lily.

He didn't have to keep on. She could dream if she wanted!

And that was all it was, thought Lily: just a beautiful dream. Luki wasn't going to stay in the past! Why would he when he had Serissa waiting for him? Serissa, the girl in the photograph. At least he wasn't still in the clutches of Dandelion Head, that was something. Serissa had looked so much nicer!

She had also, thought Lily with a jolt of surprise, looked a bit like Lily herself. Serissa had been tiny! It was one of the reasons Dandelion had sneered. *Like some kind of* doll.

Auntie Marjorie had once commented that Lily looked like a doll: 'So tiny and pretty!'

Needless to say, the Little Angel – like Dandelion – had sneered. Not just sneered: she had actually been rude enough to snigger.

A doll! Tee-hee!

Auntie Marjorie had told her off and said that Lily was 'petite'.

Whatever she was, it was neither here nor there. Luki belonged to Serissa – and Lily was going to be his great-grandmother. She couldn't even dream about him any more. Miss Carpenter would probably say that was a good thing.

We must be for ever vigilant, girls! We must not become obsessed.

She wondered if Miss Carpenter had ever been obsessed – whether she had ever had a boyfriend. Maybe, thought Lily, sadly, she should just give up thinking about boys and resign herself to being a career woman. Not that there was anything wrong with being a career woman! It seemed to make Miss Carpenter perfectly happy and contented. Not even Dad, in his silly jokey way, could accuse her of being a sour old maid. Miss Carpenter inspired people! Maybe Lily could be a teacher and inspire people. Dandelion Head might have assured her she would get married, the same as everyone else – well, almost everyone else – but who could rely on Dandelion Head? Was Dandelion Head going to do anything to help? No! She just wanted to make sure Luki didn't end up with Serissa; she didn't care what happened to Lily. For all Lily knew she might be planning something even now! It seemed she would do anything to stop Serissa being with Luki, even pushing Lily under a bus if that was what it took. There was obviously *someone* she was determined to stop Lily from meeting. The question was, who? And how, exactly, was she planning to do it?

CHAPTER
10

Glumly, at school next day, Tara informed them that, 'She's already handed out the invitations.' They didn't have to ask who 'she' was, just followed the direction of Tara's gaze to where Daniela was preening herself among a group of admirers.

'How do you actually know?' said Lily.

'Nina Kirby told me. She gave them out before assembly.'

'Oh! I wondered what they were doing,' said Lily. She had seen them all in morning assembly, secretively opening envelopes.

'So you mean we haven't been invited?' said Geraldine.

'Obviously not,' said Tara.

Well, that settled it, thought Lily. So much for meeting boys! She was obviously destined to follow in Miss Carpenter's footsteps and be a career woman.

'Told you it was a waste of time,' said Geraldine. 'All that buttering up . . . Might just as well not have bothered.'

'I dunno!' Tara never stayed down for long. 'Last year she had a second party at Christmas. So if she keeps on coming to the club—'

'And you go on buttering!'

'I'm doing what I can,' said Tara. 'At least I'm *trying*.'

'Oh, why bother? Who wants to go to her stupid party, anyway?'

'*I'd* like to,' said Lily.

They both turned to look at her. They seemed surprised.

'Didn't know you were that keen,' said Geraldine.

'Well –' She gave a little self-conscious giggle. 'All those boys . . .'

'Oodles of them,' said Tara.

'*Honestly.*' Geraldine made a tutting sound. She looked

at Tara with stern disapproval. 'You've already got one boyfriend . . . isn't that enough?'

'I was thinking of Lily. She hasn't got one.'

Lily squirmed. Geraldine rolled her eyes. 'There is life *without* boys, you know!'

'Yeah, but –' Tara gave one of her impish grins – 'it's a lot more fun with them!'

Later, to Lily, as they left school, Tara said, 'You could always come down the club one day. Lots of boys there!'

In an immediate panic Lily said, 'It's rather a long way. Either Mum or Dad would have to drive me there and then come and pick me up. It might not be convenient.'

'Well, think about it,' said Tara.

She didn't need to think about it. She had already been to a youth club. She had gone last year with a girl called Stella who lived in her road. It had been Stella's mum who had suggested it.

'Stella absolutely adores it! She's made so many new friends. She'd be more than happy to take Lily.'

Mum had said, 'Why not give it a go?'

So Lily had given it a go and spent most of the time standing in a corner clutching a glass of lemonade, too shy to talk to anyone. Everybody there knew everybody else and she hadn't known anybody at all, not even Stella, except just to say hello to, and, anyway, Stella was two years older than Lily. The woman in charge had obviously felt sorry for her. She had said, 'Hello, is this your first time? We must get you organised,' and had then been called away and hadn't come back, while Stella was busy laughing with a group of friends and seemed to have forgotten her, and the only boy who took any notice of her was jealously dragged off by some girl who obviously regarded him as her property. If Lily could have found her own way home without waiting for Stella she would have done, but they had taken so many twists and turns on the drive there that she had totally lost all sense of direction. Not that she had much to begin with. At the end of her first day at secondary school she had managed to get lost and had arrived home an hour late to find Mum on the point of ringing the police.

The fact was, thought Lily, she was just useless. Hard to imagine Miss Carpenter ever being useless. She wouldn't have stood in a corner too scared to talk to anyone. *She* wouldn't have got lost. Lily did it all the time! Dad had once said he was amazed she could even find her way from one room to another. 'Walking round with your head in the air!'

That had been on the never-to-be-forgotten occasion when she had gone to the local shops and taken a wrong turn on the way back, ending up miles from anywhere in a part of town she didn't recognise. Thomas, with brotherly scorn, had said she must have a screw loose.

Dad had chuckled and told her not to worry. 'The screws are all intact . . . She's just a bit of a dreamer. Aren't you? Eh?'

It was true; she *had* been dreaming. But Dad could chuckle all he liked – it really wasn't funny. It was utterly pathetic! It could also be quite scary, suddenly discovering you'd been walking in totally the wrong direction and had no idea where you were. Even now, she realised, as she crossed the bottom of Barclay Road on her way to school the following morning, she wasn't properly concentrating. Did everyone go around in a daze, their heads buzzing with activity? It was no wonder she kept getting lost. She wasn't safe to be let out! Imagine if there was an accident right in front of her, like someone getting run over and the police called her as a witness and she had to admit she hadn't even noticed! How shameful would that be? Especially if—

Oops! She came to a sudden halt. Standing in front of her, beaming triumphantly, was Dandelion Head.

'Not *again*,' said Lily.

'Aren't you pleased to see me? I thought you'd be pleased to see me! I thought we were friends.'

'Well, we're not,' said Lily. She was feeling hot and cross. She couldn't be bothered with Dandelion Head. 'I wish you would just leave me alone!'

'That,' said Dandelion, 'is a very hurtful thing to say. After all the risks I've run coming here!'

'I didn't ask you to come here,' said Lily. 'In fact, I'd rather you *didn't* come here.'

'Really?' Dandelion Head wrinkled her brow, as if puzzled. 'I'd have thought most people would find it quite interesting being able to talk to someone who knew what their future was going to be.'

Scornfully, Lily said, 'If I wanted to know my future, I'd go to a fortune-teller.'

'Huh! Well. You'd be lucky to find one that's genuine.'

'*Are* there any?' said Lily, sidetracked in spite of herself. She had often wondered.

'Only a handful,' said Dandelion. 'Just a few that can look into the future . . . and not by gazing at crystal balls!'

'So how? How would they do it?'

'Same as me! I could set up as a fortune-teller if I wanted. If I took a fancy to stay here. Which I wouldn't, cos who on earth would want to? I suppose there might be some who would . . . Like, if they'd been caught breaking the law and had to flee for safety.'

'Maybe you'll be caught breaking the law,' said Lily, sourly. She really was in no mood to humour Dandelion Head. 'Serve you right, for meddling with people's lives!'

'Is that what you think I'm doing?'

'Well, what do *you* think you're doing?'

'Just pulling the odd thread . . . I told you! Won't make any difference, as far as you're concerned. Anyway, I'm only here now cos I've got some news for you.'

'What?' Lily said it reluctantly, curiosity getting the better of her.

'It's good!' said Dandelion. 'You'll like it. I know you get anxious about things, like not having a boyfriend and whether you'll ever get married, which is just, like, *so* outdated, but there you go! If it's what you want . . . I'm trying to help. You don't have to look like that!'

'Like *what*?'

'All puckered and pouty.' Dandelion Head sucked in her cheeks and stuck out her lower lip. 'Wait till you hear what I've got to tell you! *You* are going to a party! How about that?'

'It's not exactly news,' said Lily. 'I know I'm going to a party! It's our neighbour's birthday. He's going to be eighty, and my mum's arranged this big gathering for him.'

'Oh! That boring old thing! That won't be any fun.'

Lily frowned. 'So what party are *you* talking about?'

'I'm talking about one with boys. Including one that I happen to know has a crush on you!'

'On me?' Lily felt her cheeks instantly break into an embarrassed beetroot glow. 'How do you know?'

'I know everything!'

'So who is it?'

'Not telling! You'll have to wait and see.'

'I might not want to go,' said Lily.

A flash of annoyance crossed Dandelion's face. 'Are you telling me all my hard work might be for nothing? I've arranged this specially for you! I thought it would make you *happy*. I thought you might be a bit grateful. Honestly,' grumbled Dandelion, 'I'm doing my best! I can't do more.

There comes a point when you have to shift for yourself. I've set things in motion – the rest is up to you!'

With that she went flouncing off. She didn't bother, this time, to fade away gradually; simply did her old trick of suddenly not being there. What a thoroughly annoying person she was! And what did she know, anyway? Couldn't even get the date right half the time! Probably talking about a party that had happened last year or the year before. Lily stomped on, crossly, on her way to school. She was sick of Dandelion Head and her constant interfering. Why couldn't she just leave Lily alone to get on with her life?

As she reached the school gates, she saw that Daniela was approaching her from the opposite direction. 'Hey, Lily!'

Lily turned. The great Daniela lowering herself to talk to her?

'Here!' Daniela held out an envelope. 'I just wanted to give you this.'

A pink envelope with balloons printed on it.

'For me?' Lily gazed at it in wonderment.

'It's an invitation to my party. We're moving house at the weekend. We're going to be living just up the road from you!'

'Really?' said Lily.

'Yup! Number twenty-eight. You're number fourteen, aren't you?'

Lily nodded.

'Mum said as we're going to be neighbours it would only be friendly to invite you. I'm sorry it's such short notice but it all happened in a bit of a rush. I hope you can come cos there's someone that'll be dead disappointed if you can't!'

Lily, immediately blushing, said, 'Oh?'

'Friend of my brother's. He's got this thing about you! Saw you last term in the school show.'

'Oh. *That*,' said Lily.

'I know!' Daniela nodded, sympathetically. 'If it hadn't been for my dad writing the music, it would have been a complete embarrassment!'

It had been a complete embarrassment with or without the music. Lily had played an elf called Twinkle. Fortunately, since she couldn't act and suffered from acute stage fright, she hadn't had any lines to speak of – just the occasional 'Yes, my lord' – but Tara, kindly, had said that at least she had looked the part.

'The tiniest person they could find!'

Tara herself had played the leader of a gang of gnomes, with loads of lines and lots of action.

'All very *silly*,' according to Geraldine, though even she had been a villager and done a bit of singing.

'So . . . this boy,' said Lily, cautiously. 'He actually came to see it?'

'Had to! Didn't have much choice. It was his auntie who did the costumes.'

Horror heaped on horror! The costumes had been almost more of an embarrassment than the show itself. Well, Lily's certainly had. A bright green leotard and big pointy ears . . . She still shuddered at the thought of it.

'Anyway,' said Daniela, 'he seemed to think you were

cute, so he asked my brother to find out who you were, and now he really, really, *really* wants to meet you, which means you've got to come or he'll never forgive me! You will come, won't you?'

She would have liked to say that she couldn't, because surely it would be disloyal going to Daniela's birthday party if Geraldine and Tara hadn't been invited? On the other hand . . . *there comes a point when you have to shift for yourself.* Dandelion Head might be a total pain, but she was right. This was an opportunity not to be missed!

CHAPTER
11

Mum was surprised when Lily told her.

'Number twenty-eight? But I thought that had been sold to a young couple with a baby? I suppose it must have fallen through.'

'Anyway,' said Lily, 'can I tell her that I'll go?'

'Of course you can! When is it?'

Lily looked at the invitation, then her face fell. 'Oh! It's the same day as Mr Peachey's birthday party!'

'Well, that's a shame,' said Mum. 'Two parties in one day! That doesn't happen very often.'

'I don't suppose—' began Lily.

She got no further. Thomas, jealously, jumped in. 'You

can't not go to Mr Peachey's party! Can she, Mum? Tell her she can't! If I have to go, she has to go!'

'No one is making you,' said Mum. 'Either of you. But it would be rather bad manners and it would really upset Mr Peachey!'

Thomas said, 'See?'

'I can't understand,' said Mum, 'why *you* wouldn't want to go. I can see that Lily might be a bit torn, but what's your problem?'

'Haven't got one,' said Thomas. 'I just don't see why she should be able to back out.'

'I'm not backing out,' said Lily.

She couldn't! Or could she? Mum did say she wasn't *making* anyone go. She was perfectly free to choose. *It's my decision*, thought Lily.

'Hey, you know what?' said Thomas.

'What?'

'I just had a horrible thought.'

Mum sighed. 'What now?'

'Didn't Uncle Nick go to Mr Peachey's school?'

Lily said, 'Oh!' She turned, aghast, to look at Mum.

'He did,' said Thomas, 'didn't he?' He said it almost accusingly, as if Mum were in some way responsible.

'He did,' agreed Mum. 'And, yes, Uncle Nick will be coming. And, yes, he will be bringing Auntie Marjorie. And, yes—'

'*Mu-u-um!*' they shouted it in unison. '*Not Smellie?*'

'Oh, don't be so silly and melodramatic,' said Mum. 'There'll be so many people there you won't even notice her!'

Apologetically, next day, Lily showed the invitation to the others. She hastened to assure them that Daniela hadn't invited her because she actually wanted to.

'She's only done it cos her mum said she had to. They're moving into our road and her mum said it would only be polite. Well, and cos her brother's friend wants to meet me.'

She couldn't resist adding the last bit.

'Why would he want to do that?' wondered Geraldine. 'Does he know you?'

Blushingly Lily explained that he had seen her in the end-of-term show.

'What, playing that Tinkle thing?'

'Twinkle,' snapped Lily.

'Sorry! Twinkle. Twinkle, twinkle, little elf—'

'He thought I looked cute.'

'I suppose you did quite.'

'Which just goes to show,' said Tara.

'Show what?' said Geraldine.

'That you just never know!'

'Doesn't matter, anyway,' said Lily. 'I'm not going to be able to go.'

'*What?*' Tara stared in outrage. Nobody turned down an invitation to Daniela's famous parties! 'You've got to!'

'So that you can tell us about it,' urged Geraldine.

'It's no good.' Lily shook her head. 'I can't! It's Mr Peachey's birthday and Mum's arranged a party for him. He's going to be eighty . . . I can't not go!'

Geraldine said, 'Mr Peachey's the one that lives next door to you, right?'

'Yes, and he's looking forward to us being there, me and Thomas. Cos we're like the grandchildren he never had.'

'Hmm.' Geraldine pulled a face. 'That's a difficult one.'

'No, it's not.' Tara said it heatedly. 'If she doesn't go to Daniela's, she might never get to meet this boy! It could be her big opportunity. I mean, let's face it,' said Tara, 'how many boys are you going to meet at the other party? It'll all be old people!'

'Not all,' said Lily.

'But *he* won't be there, will he?'

Lily had to agree that he wouldn't

'So don't you want to find out who he is and what he looks like? I would!' said Tara.

'Yes, but you're boy mad,' said Geraldine.

'I so am not! I'm just saying, it's perfectly normal. I hope you haven't told Daniela you can't go?'

'Not yet,' said Lily.

'Well, thank goodness for that! Think about it,' urged Tara.

She tried not to think about it too much during class, because of not being obsessed, but it was there all the time, niggling at her. She *did* want to find out who the boy was and what he looked like! No boy had ever had a crush on her before – not, at least, that she was aware of. And to think that Dandelion Head had known about it! *I've arranged this specially for you . . .*

If she didn't go, he might meet someone else and forget all about her. She could regret it for the rest of her life! She had a sudden vision of herself, grown old like Mr Peachey. Old and grey and all alone, sighing over missed opportunities.

She had to go! She would tell Mr Peachey that she was sorry. She would explain to him just how important it was. He would understand! He wasn't one of those crotchety old people who did nothing but complain about modern youth and how selfish they were. He had said to Lily once, when Mum had told her off for not tidying up her bedroom in spite of having been asked to at least a dozen times, 'I remember what it was like to be young . . . far better things to do than tidy bedrooms!' Mum had shaken her head in despair, but Mr Peachey had just looked at Lily and winked. He would probably tell her to 'Go and enjoy yourself! Have fun!'

In any case, she thought, there would be so many people at the party, he would be so busy catching up with all those old pupils he hadn't seen since they were boys, that he probably wouldn't even notice if Lily wasn't there. And, besides, there was always the Little Angel to fill the gap, prancing and twirling and doing her party pieces, singing 'Happy Birthday to You' in her loud, penetrating voice. Thomas, of course, would sulk.

Mum would probably look at her reproachfully, but Lily would assure her that she had spoken to Mr Peachey and that he had given her his blessing. She wouldn't say anything about Daniela's brother having a friend who wanted to meet her because Thomas would be bound to make some sort of rude scoffing noise, and Mum might not be altogether sympathetic. She probably wouldn't regard meeting boys as a good enough reason for not going to Mr Peachey's party. Dad might be a bit more understanding, but she would find it embarrassing telling Dad in case he laughed. 'How about that, then? Our Lily's got a secret admirer!'

Dad would laugh, Thomas would be resentful, Mum would try to make her feel guilty. But one way or another, thought Lily, she had to get to that party!

Maybe, she thought, as she made her way home after school, she could call in and see Mr Peachey right away, before feelings of guilt could set in. Not, she argued, that there was anything to feel guilty about. She would make Mr Peachey a birthday card, hand-painted, *To a beloved Grandad on his 80th birthday*. He would like that! And she would give him the present she had made – a small pottery jar with a lid. She was proud of her pottery jar! She had made it in art, last term, especially for Mr Peachey's birthday. She was going to fill it with big stripy humbugs, his favourite sweets.

If she was going to speak to him, thought Lily, she must obviously be brave and do it immediately. It wouldn't be fair to Mr Peachey to leave it till the last moment. Taking a deep breath, she marched up the path and knocked at Mr Peachey's door.

There was no reply.

Bother, thought Lily. Just when she needed him to be there!

She knocked again in case he was upstairs, but there was still no reply. Bother, bother, bother! Her courage would evaporate if she didn't speak to him soon.

She went back down the path and into her own garden, only to find Mr Peachey sitting in the kitchen with Mum. He had one of his legs propped on a chair, and Mum was rubbing arnica cream into his ankle.

'What's happened?' cried Lily, depositing her school bag with a thud on the floor.

'Nothing to worry about,' said Mr Peachey. 'Silly old man had a bit of an accident, that's all. Fell off the edge of the kerb! Crocked the old ankle. Stupid thing to do!'

'At least it's not broken,' said Mum. 'Just bruised. Still, you'll need to take it easy for a day or two.'

'But what about the party?' said Lily.

'Oh, don't you worry about the party! I'll be there for that.'

'You don't think –' Lily turned hopefully to Mum – 'you don't think we ought to postpone it for a while?'

'You'll do no such thing!' Mr Peachey sounded outraged. 'Postpone my party? I never heard the like!' He winked at Lily to show he wasn't really angry. 'Take more than a bit of a tumble to keep this old bird down! The fates might have intended otherwise, but they obviously don't know who they're dealing with. Push a poor old fellow off the kerb, do his ankle in . . . Might work with some folk, but not this one!'

Lily puckered her brow. 'Are you saying someone pushed you?'

'I only wish I could! I'm afraid it was more likely just me missing my footing. These things happen, you know, when you get to my great age. Anyway, no need to worry! I'll be there to cut my cake and have a birthday hug.'

Dear Daniela, wrote Lily, sadly, *I am very sorry that I cannot come to your birthday party. Thank you very much for inviting me. I really would have liked to come. I hope you have a lovely time.*

'Well, that's a bore,' said Tara, when Lily showed her what she had written. 'I wanted to know who this person is that has a thing for you! And about the party! I wanted to know what the party would be like!'

'Yes, so did I,' said Geraldine. 'Just out of curiosity. And now she's not going!'

They turned, rather accusingly, to look at Lily.

Tara said, 'How can you *do* this to us? After I've worked and worked at it!'

'All that buttering up,' said Geraldine. 'All for nothing!'

Spiritedly, Lily said, 'Not my fault she didn't ask you two!'

She refused to be made to feel guilty. She couldn't

let Mr Peachey down, and that was all there was to it. Dandelion Head would no doubt be cross after (so she claimed) all her efforts, but then Dandelion was cross about most things. Maybe now she would go away and leave Lily alone. That, thought Lily, would be something. Even if she didn't get to meet boys – even if Tara was right, and Daniela's brother's friend found someone else to have a crush on – at least she would be rid of that tiresome, bossy, meddling girl.

It wasn't much consolation. In fact, it wasn't really any consolation at all. She only knew that she couldn't bring herself to hurt Mr Peachey. He was so looking forward to his birthday hug!

'You're going to make an old man very happy,' said Mum, as they prepared, on Saturday evening, to leave for the party. 'Both of you!'

CHAPTER
12

The party was being held in a room above a local restaurant. It was a large room – 'Meant for banquets,' said Mum – and to begin with there were only a handful of people there. But then, very quickly, it began to fill up, until there was quite a crowd, all arriving in groups, bearing lots of exciting-looking parcels and packages which they left on a table just inside the door.

Mr Peachey said, 'Goodness me!'

'It's all your old pupils,' said Lily. 'Mum wrote and invited them! She wanted it to be a surprise.'

'It's that all right,' said Mr Peachey. 'Goodness gracious! However many are coming?'

'Lots,' said Lily. 'Cos you were very popular. Do you recognise any of them?'

'I do, indeed! There's that scamp that used to cause me so much trouble – Billy Wilson! Oh, have I got a bone to pick with him, the rascal!'

Lily giggled as Mr Peachey made his way slowly across the room to where a tall distinguished-looking man was talking to Mum. After a few more words Mum left them together and came over to Lily.

'Well, you'll never believe it,' she said. 'That's a high court judge!'

'He's called Billy Wilson,' said Lily, 'and Mr Peachey has gone to pick a bone with him.'

'Really?'

Lily nodded. 'He's a rascal.'

'Well, I never,' said Mum. 'Thomas!' She beckoned him over. 'Tell me you're enjoying yourself?'

'Yeah, it's okay,' said Thomas. 'Gotta go!'

Mum and Lily stood watching as Thomas rushed back to a group of boys gathered in a corner.

'Hmm! It didn't take him long,' said Mum. 'How about you? I'm sure you could find someone to talk to if you looked around. Melanie, for instance. I just saw her come in. Why don't you go and talk to her?'

'Mum, *please*.'

Talk to Melanie in her horrible pink dress with the big bunchy skirt? She would rather die!

'Well, you can't just stand here by yourself! Your brother's obviously found some chums. Why not go and join them?'

'Because they're all about nine years old,' said Lily.

'Oh, I don't know,' said Mum. 'One of them looks a bit older than that.'

Lily said, 'Mum, I'm all right!'

Mum, obviously not happy, shook her head and went off, leaving Lily standing there. Lily thought, *I am always like this at parties.* Even if she had been able to go to Daniela's she would probably only have hidden away in a corner all night, too tongue-tied to speak.

She felt a hand on her shoulder and jumped round.

It was Mr Peachey, back from picking a bone with the high court judge.

'Did you tell him off?' said Lily.

'Oh, I did! Believe me.'

'He doesn't look as if it bothered him very much.'

'I told you, he's a rascal. But look here, young lady! Why do I find you skulking about on your own?'

'It's what I do,' said Lily. 'I like to watch people.'

'Not at my party, you don't! Not when there's a rather handsome young gentleman over there who's obviously desperate to be introduced.'

Lily spun round. A pair of piercing blue eyes met hers. Bright blue eyes and curly black hair . . . Her cheeks instantly went into full beetroot mode.

'Come!' Mr Peachey put a hand beneath her elbow. 'Let me do the honours.' He shepherded her across the room. The boy with the blue eyes was now looking every bit as embarrassed as Lily herself.

'Now, correct me if I'm wrong,' said Mr Peachey, 'but you must be Bernard Meldrum's son. Am I right?'

The boy said, 'Yes, sir. Lucas Meldrum, sir.'

'Let me introduce you to my granddaughter, Lily. Can't have you both standing about on your own! What kind of party would that be? You get talking while I see if I can locate your father.'

'He's over there,' said Lucas, pointing. 'Would you like me to go and get him for you?'

'No, I'd like you to stay right here,' said Mr Peachey, 'and entertain my granddaughter!'

He hobbled off, leaving them to stand in awkward silence, both too bashful to say anything. And then, all of a sudden, a loud screeching filled the room.

'On the go-o-o-o-d ship
LOLLIPOP—'

In startled tones Lucas said, 'What in God's name is that?'

Lily giggled. 'That's my cousin!'

'Oh.' He looked even more embarrassed. 'Sorry!'

'That's all right,' said Lily. 'She's a pain. Her name's Melanie . . . We call her the Little Angel.'

'Doesn't sound much like an angel!'

They both winced as the shrieking turned into a high-pitched scream.

'I expect she'll start dancing in a minute,' said Lily.

Lucas said, 'Blimey!'

'There she goes,' said Lily. The sound of vigorous clicking and clacking could be heard as the Little Angel's tap shoes made their way across the floor. 'Apparently,' said Lily, 'she's very good at it.'

'If you like that kind of thing.'

'I normally do,' said Lily, trying to be fair. 'If it's on stage. Not so much when it's at someone else's party.'

'Just have to hope your grandad likes it.'

'My grand— Oh! Mr Peachey. He isn't really my grandad,' said Lily. 'He's our next-door neighbour. We've known him for ever. He always says that me and Thomas are like the grandchildren he never had.'

'Ah.' Lucas nodded. 'I thought I remembered my dad saying he didn't have any family.'

'Only us,' said Lily. 'We're his family. That's why my mum organised the party for him.'

'It's a good party, too! I'm glad now that I came. I almost didn't.'

Lily said, 'Really?'

'Got asked to something else at the last minute by my friend Tony. He wanted me to go with him and his dad to this old car museum.'

Gravely, Lily said, 'Would you rather have gone there?'

'Yeah!' His eyes gleamed. 'It's got all these really ancient cars from way back. We were supposed to be going last weekend but Tony's dad had a bit of an accident, fell off a ladder and busted his arm.'

Mr Peachey had had a bit of an accident, too. Lily frowned. 'It's funny,' she said. 'I almost didn't come either.'

That meddlesome interfering Dandelion Head! She must have pulled threads all over the place. Poor Mr

Peachey spraining his ankle, Lucas's friend's dad falling off a ladder, even Daniela, suddenly moving into Lily's road and inviting Lily to her party. She had obviously been responsible for all of it! Just to stop Lily from bumping into Lucas . . . She had wondered who it was that Dandelion had been so desperate for her not to meet. Now she knew! Dandelion had done all she could to keep them apart, trying to get Lily to go to a different party, trying to send Lucas off to an old car museum. Well, so much for her and her attempts to change the timeline! It was too late, now. They had met anyway!

She became aware that Lucas was looking at her, expectantly. 'So why did *you* almost not come?'

'It was this girl at school,' said Lily. 'Invited me to her birthday party. She's never asked me before. Not ever! I would have loved to have gone cos her dad's a quite famous singer, and everybody, but *everybody*, wants to be invited to her parties, but – you know! I'd promised Mr Peachey. It wouldn't have been fair to let him down.'

'That's what my dad said. He said Mr Peachey didn't

have any family, and that people that had been his pupils owed everything to him, and it was up to them to come along and bring *their* families and show him how much he meant to them. I *could* have gone to the museum. Dad said he wouldn't make me come with him if I really didn't want to. But somehow I just couldn't do it.'

'Me neither,' said Lily.

'Of course, there's so many people here he probably wouldn't have missed us. But then . . .' There was a pause. Lucas, suddenly grown rather pink, said, 'Then I wouldn't have got to meet you!'

Lily, by now also rather pink, mumbled, 'And I wouldn't have got to meet you!'

'When you think of it, it's an extraordinary coincidence both of us almost not turning up!'

'Sort of like fate,' said Lily.

'Do you believe in fate?' He looked at her, earnestly. 'I reckon we have free will. If we'd left it to fate, we might not have come. Either of us! I might be walking around an old car museum right now.'

And I might be at Daniela's party, thought Lily. *Meeting lots of boys and being too shy to say anything to them.*

'Which would you rather?' said Lucas. 'Be here or at your other party?'

'Be here!' said Lily. And then, feeling suddenly bold: 'Where would *you* rather be? Here or at your car museum?'

He grinned. 'What do you think?'

'I don't know,' said Lily. 'That's why I'm asking!'

The church clock across the way was striking the hour as Mr Peachey appeared to say that he was about to cut his cake and needed Lily there to witness it.

'See me blow out my candles! All eighty of them!'

'*Eighty?*' Lucas sounded impressed. 'How do you fit eighty candles on a birthday cake?'

'You'll see! Come along, come along! Enough chitchat.'

Mr Peachey put a hand on Lily's shoulder and piloted her firmly across the room. 'And you, young man!'

Lucas followed, obediently. They had been talking, Lily realised, with something of a start, for almost fifteen minutes. Fifteen minutes talking to a boy! It had been so easy. She hadn't had to rack her brains for what to say – just opened her mouth and let the words spill out. They had talked about anything and everything. She had learnt that Lucas lived locally, that he went to St Andrew's, that he had a dog called Monty and a baby sister called Lisa – and that his mum, embarrassingly, sometimes referred to him as Luki.

'But only when she's feeling soppy! I mean, it's a pretty soppy kind of name, anyway, *Lucas*.' He screwed up his face. 'It's my dad's name, *and* my grandad's. If ever I have a son, they'll probably expect me to call him Lucas as well.'

'I think it's nice,' said Lily. 'I think Luki's quite nice, too . . . better than *Lil*!'

Not that anyone ever called her Lil, but once she had started, words just seemed to come tumbling out of her. She had told Lucas all kinds of things she had never told anyone before. How she wanted more than anything to be an inspiration like Miss Carpenter but hadn't yet been able to work out what sort of thing she could do to inspire anyone, since she wasn't clever like Geraldine, who was aiming for university, or talented like Tara, who was going to be an actress. How she really, really hated it when people like Auntie Marjorie said she looked like a doll, because no one that looked like a doll was ever going to be taken seriously, and she was hoping that maybe soon she would have what her mum called 'a growth spurt' and suddenly shoot up like a beanpole.

Lucas had assured her that *he* took her seriously and promised that he wouldn't ever say she looked like a doll so long as she promised not to call him Luki.

'Ever! That is—'

At that point he had broken off and become rather pink again. 'That is,' he had mumbled, 'if the occasion should ever arise.'

'You mean –' Lily had said it carefully, anxious not to be misunderstood – 'you mean if we happened to see each other again?'

Lucas, by now bright scarlet, had said that you never knew.

'Could easily bump into each other, just walking about.'

Greatly daring, Lily said, ''Specially as we live so close.'

'Yeah!' His face lit up. 'We do, don't we?'

'Just a few minutes away, really.'

'Dunno how we've never met before.'

Don't know how we managed to meet at all, thought Lily, vengefully. It was no thanks to Dandelion Head! It made her go quite cold to think how close she had come to asking Mr Peachey if he would mind her going to Daniela's party instead of his. He would almost certainly have told her that of course she should go. If he had been at home when she tried to speak to him, rather than sitting in Mum's kitchen having his ankle bandaged, she would have gone racing off to Daniela's and she and Lucas might never have met.

Dandelion Head had certainly messed *that* one up! Served her right, making people fall off ladders and pushing old men off the kerb. She jolly well deserved it if Luki ended up with Serissa. Which, according to Dandelion, meant that Lily became Luki's great-grandmother, which meant that Lily and Lucas . . .

'Penny for your thoughts?'

She wouldn't have told him for the world! Luckily, she was spared having to think of something to say by Mr Peachey arriving and telling them that they had had enough chitchat. 'I'm going to blow out my candles!'

Before Mr Peachey could blow out his candles they had to suffer the Little Angel squawking her way through 'Happy Birthday'. Lucas caught Lily's eye and pulled a face, making Lily splutter and dissolve into giggles. The Little Angel, whose beady eyes never missed a trick, shot a furious look at her across the room.

'Now I'll be for it,' whispered Lily.

Lucas let his hand steal into hers and give it a squeeze. 'Don't worry, I'll protect you!'

She giggled again at that. Mum gave her a slight frown and a shake of the head, but Lily could tell she wasn't really cross. Thomas, meanwhile, was grinning broadly.

'I saw you!' he said, as half an hour later the party began to break up. 'I saw who you were talking to!'

Lucas, on his way through the door accompanied by his dad, turned and waved. Lily, blushing, waved back.

The Little Angel stared, jealously. 'Who was that?'

'What's it to you?' said Thomas.

Mum said, 'Thomas!'

'Well, what business is it of hers?' said Thomas.

The Little Angel, in an aggrieved shriek, informed him that she was only asking. 'I suppose a person can *ask*?'

'Whoever he was,' said Mum, 'he seemed a very nice boy.'

Lily muttered that his dad had been one of Mr Peachey's old pupils.

'So now you know,' said Thomas. He gave Lily a sly nudge. '*The whole evening!*'

The Little Angel said, 'It's very rude, isn't it, Mum, to come to a party and just stand and talk to one person all the time?'

Auntie Marjorie, gently rebuking, said, 'Hush, Mellie! Not now.'

'But I thought we were supposed to be *sociable*! I wouldn't call it very sociable to just stand and talk to the same person all the time. *I* wouldn't just stand and talk to one person!'

Thomas said, 'No, you'd just—'

'*Thomas!*' Mum gave him a shove. 'Time we were going. I'm sure Mr Peachey's feeling in need of a bit of peace and quiet. Come along, the pair of you!'

Mum shepherded them both outside, where Dad was waiting for them by the car, with Mr Peachey, looking weary but happy, already in his seat.

'*Holding hands*,' hissed Thomas, as he and Lily climbed into the back after Mum. 'I saw!'

'Yes,' said Mum on the phone with Auntie Marjorie a few days later, 'it was a huge success! Mr Peachey was so grateful. And, yes, in reply to your question, I do believe that love is in the air . . .'

Lily, on the point of entering the room, froze in the doorway.

'I watched them the other day,' said Mum, 'her and her young man walking up the road together, holding hands like they were soulmates already!'

Soulmates, thought Lily. That was what they were: soulmates! And maybe one day, after all, in spite of Dandelion Head and her meddling, she would be Luki's great-grandmother just as she was supposed to be. And Dandelion Head could just go and – and *boil* herself!

A heartwarming animal
adventure about the power
of friendship

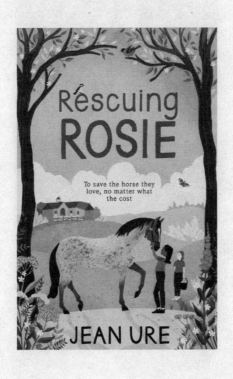

A tale of dancing and following your dreams

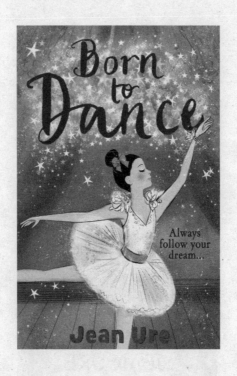

A story of crushes, first love
and friendship

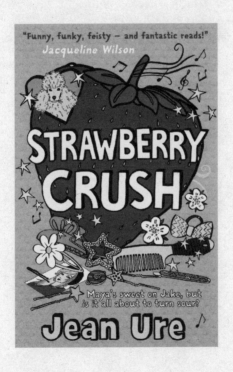